The Story of the Gadsby

Rudyard Kipling

Contents

THE STORY OF THE GADSBY

BY

Rudyard Kipling

Preface

To THE ADDRESS OF

CAPTAIN J. MAFFLIN,

Duke of Derry's (Pink) Hussars.

DEAR MAFFLIN,--You will remember that I wrote this story as an Awful Warning. None the less you have seen fit to disregard it and have followed Gadsby's example--as I betted you would. I acknowledge that you paid the money at once, but you have prejudiced the mind of Mrs. Mafflin against myself, for though I am almost the only respectable friend of your bachelor days, she has been darwaza band to me throughout the season. Further, she caused you to invite me to dinner at the Club, where you called me "a wild ass of the desert," and went home at half-past ten, after discoursing for twenty minutes on the responsibilities of housekeeping. You now drive a mail-phaeton and sit under a Church of England clergyman. I am not angry, Jack. It is your kismet, as it was Gaddy's, and his kismet who can avoid? Do not think that I am moved by a spirit of revenge as I write, thus publicly, that you and you alone are responsible for this book. In other and more expansive days, when you could look at a magnum without flushing and at a cheroot without turning white, you supplied me with most of the material. Take it back again--would that I could have preserved your fatherless speech in the telling--take it back, and by your slippered hearth read it to the late Miss Deercourt. She will not be any the more willing to receive my cards, but she will admire you immensely, and you, I feel sure, will love me. You may even invite me to another very bad dinner--at the Club, which, as you and your wife know, is a safe neutral ground for the entertainment of wild asses. Then, my very dear hypocrite, we shall be quits.

Yours always,

RUDYARD KIPLING.

P. S.--On second thoughts I should recommend you to keep the book away from Mrs. Mafflin.

POOR DEAR MAMMA

The wild hawk to the wind-swept sky, The deer to the wholesome wold, And
the heart of a man to the heart of a maid, As it was in the days of old.
Gypsy Song.

SCENE.--Interior of Miss MINNIE THREEGAN'S Bedroom at Simla. Miss
THREEGAN, in window-seat, turning over a drawerful of things. Miss
EMMA
DEERCOURT, bosom--friend, who has come to spend the day, sitting on
the bed, manipulating the bodice of a ballroom frock, and a bunch
of artificial lilies of the valley. Time, 5:30 P. M. on a hot May
afternoon.

Miss DEERCOURT. And he said: "I shall never forget this dance," and,
of course, I said: "Oh, how can you be so silly!" Do you think he meant
anything, dear?

Miss THREEGAN. (Extracting long lavender silk stocking from the
rubbish.) You know him better than I do.

Miss D. Oh, do be sympathetic, Minnie! I'm sure he does. At least I
would be sure if he wasn't always riding with that odious Mrs. Hagan.

Miss T. I suppose so. How does one manage to dance through one's heels
first? Look at this--isn't it shameful? (Spreads stocking--heel on open

hand for inspection.)

Miss D. Never mind that! You can't mend it. Help me with this hateful bodice. I've run the string so, and I've run the string so, and I can't make the fulness come right. Where would you put this? (Waves lilies of the valley.)

Miss T. As high up on the shoulder as possible.

Miss D. Am I quite tall enough? I know it makes May Older look lopsided.

Miss T. Yes, but May hasn't your shoulders. Hers are like a hock-bottle.

BEARER. (Rapping at door.) Captain Sahib aya.

Miss D. (Jumping up wildly, and hunting for bodice, which she has discarded owing to the heat of the day.) Captain Sahib! What Captain Sahib? Oh, good gracious, and I'm only half dressed! Well, I sha'n't bother.

Miss T. (Calmly.) You needn't. It isn't for us. That's Captain Gadsby. He is going for a ride with Mamma. He generally comes five days out of the seven.

AGONIZED VOICE. (Prom an inner apartment.) Minnie, run out and give Captain Gadsby some tea, and tell him I shall be ready in ten minutes; and, O Minnie, come to me an instant, there's a dear girl!

Miss T. Oh, bother! (Aloud.) Very well, Mamma.

Exit, and reappears, after five minutes, flushed, and rubbing her fingers.

Miss D. You look pink. What has happened?

Miss T. (In a stage whisper.) A twenty-four-inch waist, and she won't let it out. Where are my bangles? (Rummager on the toilet-table, and dabs at her hair with a brush in the interval.)

Miss D. Who is this Captain Gadsby? I don't think I've met him.

Miss T. You must have. He belongs to the Harrar set. I've danced with him, but I've never talked to him. He's a big yellow man, just like a newly-hatched chicken, with an enormous moustache. He walks like this (imitates Cavalry swagger), and he goes "Ha--Hmmm!" deep down in his throat when he can't think of anything to say. Mamma likes him. I don't.

Miss D. (Abstractedly.) Does he wax that moustache?

Miss T. (Busy with Powder-puff.) Yes, I think so. Why?

Miss D. (Bending over the bodice and sewing furiously.) Oh, nothing--only--Miss T. (Sternly.) Only what? Out with it, Emma.

Miss D. Well, May Olger--she's engaged to Mr. Charteris, you know--said--Promise you won't repeat this?

Miss T. Yes, I promise. What did she say?

Miss D. That--that being kissed (with a rush) with a man who didn't wax his moustache was--like eating an egg without salt.

Miss T. (At her full height, with crushing scorn.) May Olger is a horrid, nasty Thing, and you can tell her I said so. I'm glad she doesn't belong to my set--I must go and feed this man! Do I look presentable?

Miss D. Yes, perfectly. Be quick and hand him over to your Mother, and then we can talk. I shall listen at the door to hear what you say to him.

Miss T. 'Sure I don't care. I'm not afraid of Captain Gadsby.

In proof of this swings into the drawing-room with a mannish stride followed by two short steps, which Produces the effect of a restive horse entering. Misses CAPTAIN GADSBY, who is sitting in the shadow of the window-curtain, and gazes round helplessly.

CAPTAIN GADSBY. (Aside.) The filly, by Jove! 'Must ha' picked up that action from the sire. (Aloud, rising.) Good evening, Miss Threegan.

Miss T. (Conscious that she is flushing.) Good evening, Captain Gadsby. Mamma told me to say that she will be ready in a few minutes. Won't you have some tea? (Aside.) I hope Mamma will be quick. What am I to say to the creature? (Aloud and abruptly.) Milk and sugar?

CAPT. G. No sugar, tha-anks, and very little milk. Ha--Hmmm.

Miss T. (Aside.) If he's going to do that, I'm lost. I shall laugh. I know I shall!

CAPT. G. (Pulling at his moustache and watching it sideways down his nose.) Ha--Hamm. (Aside.) 'Wonder what the little beast can talk about. 'Must make a shot at it.

Miss T. (Aside.) Oh, this is agonizing. I must say something.

Both Together. Have you Been--CAPT. G. I beg your pardon. You were going to say--Miss T. (Who has been watching the moustache with awed fascination.) Won't you have some eggs?

CAPT. G. (Looking bewilderedly at the tea-table.) Eggs! (Aside.) O Hades! She must have a nursery-tea at this hour. S'pose they've wiped her mouth and sent her to me while the Mother is getting on her duds. (Aloud.) No, thanks.

Miss T. (Crimson with confusion.) Oh! I didn't mean that. I wasn't thinking of mou--eggs for an instant. I mean salt. Won't you have some sa--sweets? (Aside.) He'll think me a raving lunatic. I wish Mamma would come.

CAPT. G. (Aside.) It was a nursery-tea and she's ashamed of it. By Jove! She doesn't look half bad when she colors up like that. (Aloud, helping himself from the dish.) Have you seen those new chocolates at Peliti's?

Miss T. No, I made these myself. What are they like?

CAPT. G. These! De-licious. (Aside.) And that's a fact.

Miss T. (Aside.) Oh, bother! he'll think I'm fishing for compliments. (Aloud.) No, Peliti's of course.

CAPT. G. (Enthusiastically.) Not to compare with these. How d'you make them? I can't get my khansamah to understand the simplest thing beyond mutton and fowl.

Miss T. Yes? I'm not a khansamah, you know. Perhaps you frighten him. You should never frighten a servant. He loses his head. It's very bad policy.

CAPT. G. He's so awf'ly stupid.

Miss T. (Folding her hands in her Zap.) You should call him quietly and say: "O khansamah jee!"

CAPT. G. (Getting interested.) Yes? (Aside.) Fancy that little featherweight saying, "O khansamah jee" to my bloodthirsty Mir Khan!

Miss T Then you should explain the dinner, dish by dish.

CAPT. G. But I can't speak the vernacular.

Miss T. (Patronizingly.) You should pass the Higher Standard and try.

CAPT. G. I have, but I don't seem to be any the wiser. Are you?

Miss T. I never passed the Higher Standard. But the khansamah is very patient with me. He doesn't get angry when I talk about sheep's topees, or order maunds of grain when I mean seers.

CAPT. G. (Aside with intense indignation.) I'd like to see Mir Khan being rude to that girl! Hullo! Steady the Buffs! (Aloud.) And do you understand about horses, too?

Miss T. A little--not very much. I can't doctor them, but I know what they ought to eat, and I am in charge of our stable.

CAPT. G. Indeed! You might help me then. What ought a man to give his sais in the Hills? My ruffian says eight rupees, because everything is so dear.

Miss T. Six rupees a month, and one rupee Simla allowance--neither more nor less. And a grass-cut gets six rupees. That's better than buying grass in the bazar.

CAPT. G. (Admiringly.) How do you know?

Miss T. I have tried both ways.

CAPT. G. Do you ride much, then? I've never seen you on the Mall.

Miss T. (Aside.) I haven't passed him more than fifty times. (Aloud.) Nearly every day.

CAPT. G. By Jove! I didn't know that. Ha--Hamm (Pulls at his moustache and is silent for forty seconds.) Miss T. (Desperately, and wondering what will happen next.) It looks beautiful. I shouldn't touch it if I were you. (Aside.) It's all Mamma's fault for not coming before. I will be rude!

CAPT. G. (Bronzing under the tan and bringing down his hand very quickly.) Eh! What-at! Oh, yes! Ha! Ha! (Laughs uneasily.) (Aside.) Well, of all the dashed cheek! I never had a woman say that to me yet. She must be a cool hand or else--Ah! that nursery-tea!

VOICE PROM THE UNKNOWN. Tchk! Tchk! Tchk!

CAPT. G. Good gracious! What's that?

Miss T. The dog, I think. (Aside.) Emma has been listening, and I'll never forgive her!

CAPT. G. (Aside.) They don't keep dogs here. (Aloud.) 'Didn't sound like a dog, did it?

Miss T. Then it must have been the cat. Let's go into the veranda. What a lovely evening it is!

Steps into veranda and looks out across the hills into sunset. The CAPTAIN follows.

CAPT. G. (Aside.) Superb eyes! I wonder that I never noticed them before! (Aloud.) There's going to be a dance at Viceregal Lodge on Wednesday. Can you spare me one?

Miss T. (Shortly.) No! I don't want any of your charity-dances. You only ask me because Mamma told you to. I hop and I bump. You know I do!

CAPT. G. (Aside.) That's true, but little girls shouldn't understand these things. (Aloud.) No, on my word, I don't. You dance beautifully.

Miss T. Then why do you always stand out after half a dozen turns? I thought officers in the Army didn't tell fibs.

CAPT. G. It wasn't a fib, believe me. I really do want the pleasure of a dance with you.

Miss T. (Wickedly.) Why? Won't Mamma dance with you any more?

CAPT. G. (More earnestly than the necessity demands.) I wasn't thinking of your Mother. (Aside.) You little vixen!

Miss T. (Still looking out of the window.) Eh? Oh, I beg your par don. I was thinking of something else.

CAPT. G. (Aside.) Well! I wonder what she'll say next. I've never known a woman treat me like this before. I might be--Dash it, I might be an Infantry subaltern! (Aloud.) Oh, please don't trouble. I'm not worth thinking about. Isn't your Mother ready yet?

Miss T. I should think so; but promise me, Captain Gadsby, you won't take poor dear Mamma twice round Jakko any more. It tires her so.

CAPT. G. She says that no exercise tires her.

Miss T. Yes, but she suffers afterward. You don't know what rheumatism is, and you oughtn't to keep her out so late, when it gets chill in the evenings.

CAPT. G. (Aside.) Rheumatism. I thought she came off her horse rather in a bunch. Whew! One lives and learns. (Aloud.) I'm sorry to hear that. She hasn't mentioned it to me.

Miss T. (Flurried.) Of course not! Poor dear Mamma never would. And you mustn't say that I told you either. Promise me that you won't. Oh, CAPTAIN Gadsby, promise me you won't!

CAPT. G. I am dumb, or--I shall be as soon as you've given me that dance, and another--if you can trouble yourself to think about me for a minute.

Miss T. But you won't like it one little bit. You'll be awfully sorry afterward.

CAPT. G. I shall like it above all things, and I shall only be sorry that I didn't get more. (Aside.) Now what in the world am I saying?

Miss T. Very well. You will have only yourself to thank if your toes are trodden on. Shall we say Seven?

CAPT. G. And Eleven. (Aside.) She can't be more than eight stone, but, even then, it's an absurdly small foot. (Looks at his own riding boots.)

Miss T. They're beautifully shiny. I can almost see my face in them.

CAPT. G. I was thinking whether I should have to go on crutches for the rest of my life if you trod on my toes.

Miss T. Very likely. Why not change Eleven for a square?

CAPT. G. No, please! I want them both waltzes. Won't you write them down?

Miss T. J don't get so many dances that I shall confuse them. You will be the offender.

CAPT. G. Wait and see! (Aside.) She doesn't dance perfectly, perhaps, but--

Miss T. Your tea must have got cold by this time. Won't you have another cup?

CAPT. G. No, thanks. Don't you think it's pleasanter out in the veranda? (Aside.) I never saw hair take that color in the sunshine before. (Aloud.) It's like one of Dicksee's pictures.

Miss T. Yes I It's a wonderful sunset, isn't it? (Bluntly.) But what do you know about Dicksee's pictures?

CAPT. G. I go Home occasionally. And I used to know the Galleries. (Nervously.) You mustn't think me only a Philistine with--a moustache.

Miss T. Don't! Please don't. I'm so sorry for what I said then. I was horribly rude. It slipped out before I thought. Don't you know the temptation to say frightful and shocking things just for the mere sake of saying them? I'm afraid I gave way to it.

CAPT. G. (Watching the girl as she flushes.) I think I know the feeling. It would be terrible if we all yielded to it, wouldn't it? For instance, I might say--POOR DEAR MAMMA. (Entering, habited, hatted, and booted.) Ah, Captain Gadsby? 'Sorry to keep you waiting. 'Hope you haven't been bored. 'My little girl been talking to you?

Miss T. (Aside.) I'm not sorry I spoke about the rheumatism. I'm not! I'm NOT! I only wished I'd mentioned the corns too.

CAPT. G. (Aside.) What a shame! I wonder how old she is. It never occurred to me before. (Aloud.) We've been discussing "Shakespeare and the musical glasses" in the veranda.

Miss T. (Aside.) Nice man! He knows that quotation. He isn't a Philistine with a moustache. (Aloud.) Good-bye, Captain Gadsby. (Aside.) What a huge hand and what a squeeze! I don't suppose he meant it, but he has driven the rings into my fingers.

POOR DEAR MAMMA. Has Vermillion come round yet? Oh, yes! Captain Gadsby,
don't you think that the saddle is too far forward? (They pass into the front veranda.)

CAPT. G. (Aside.) How the dickens should I know what she prefers? She told me that she doted on horses. (Aloud.) I think it is.

Miss T. (Coming out into front veranda.) Oh! Bad Buldoo! I must speak to him for this. He has taken up the curb two links, and Vermillion bates that. (Passes out and to horse's head.)

CAPT. G. Let me do it!

Miss. T. No, Vermillion understands me. Don't you, old man? (Looses curb-chain skilfully, and pats horse on nose and throttle.) Poor Vermillion! Did they want to cut his chin off? There!

Captain Gadsby watches the interlude with undisguised admiration.

POOR DEAR MAMMA. (Tartly to Miss T.) You've forgotten your guest, I think, dear.

Miss T. Good gracious! So I have! Good-bye. (Retreats indoors hastily.)

POOR DEAR MAMMA. (Bunching reins in fingers hampered by too tight gauntlets.) CAPTAIN Gadsby!

CAPTAIN GADSBY stoops and makes the foot-rest. POOR DEAR MAMMA blunders,
halts too long, and breaks through it.

CAPT. G. (Aside.) Can't hold up even stone forever. It's all your rheumatism. (Aloud.) Can't imagine why I was so clumsy. (Aside.) Now Little Featherweight would have gone up like a bird.

They ride oat of the garden. The Captain falls back.

CAPT. G. (Aside.) How that habit catches her under the arms! Ugh!

POOR DEAR MAMMA. (With the worn smile of sixteen seasons, the worse for
exchange.) You're dull this afternoon, CAPTAIN Gadsby.

CAPT. G. (Spurring up wearily.) Why did you keep me waiting so long?

Et cetera, et cetera, et cetera.

(AN INTERVAL OF THREE WEEKS.)

GILDED YOUTH. (Sitting on railings opposite Town Hall.) Hullo, Gandy! 'Been trotting out the Gorgonzola! We all thought it was the Gorgan you're mashing.

CAPT. G. (With withering emphasis.) You young cub! What the--does it matter to you?

Proceeds to read GILDED YOUTH a lecture on discretion and deportment, which crumbles latter like a Chinese Lantern. Departs fuming.

(FURTHER INTERVAL OF FIVE WEEKS.) SCENE.--Exterior of New Simla Library

on a foggy evening. Miss THREECAN and Miss DEERCOURT meet among the
'rickshaws. Miss T. is carrying a bundle of books under her left arm.

Miss D. (Level intonation.) Well?

Miss 'I'. (Ascending intonation.) Well?

Miss D. (Capturing her friend's left arm, taking away all the books, placing books in 'rickshaw, returning to arm, securing hand by third finger and investigating.) Well! You bad girl! And you never told me.

Miss T. (Demurely.) He--he--he only spoke yesterday afternoon.

Miss D. Bless you, dear! And I'm to be bridesmaid, aren't I? You know you promised ever so long ago.

Miss T. Of course. I'll tell you all about it to-morrow. (Gets into 'rickshaw.) O Emma!

Miss D. (With intense interest.) Yes, dear?

Miss T. (Piano.) It's quite true---- about--the--egg.

Miss D. What egg?

Miss T. (Pianissimo prestissimo.) The egg without the salt. (Porte.) Chalo ghar ko jaldi, jhampani! (Go home, jhampani.)

THE WORLD WITHOUT

Certain people of importance.

SCENE.--Smoking-room of the Degchi Club. Time, 10.30 P. M. of a stuffy night in the Rains. Four men dispersed in picturesque attitudes and easy-chairs. To these enter BLAYNE of the Irregular Moguls, in evening dress.

BLAYNE. Phew! The Judge ought to be hanged in his own store-godown. Hi, khitmatgarl Poora whiskey-peg, to take the taste out of my mouth.

CURTISS. (Royal Artillery.) That's it, is it? What the deuce made you dine at the Judge's? You know his bandobust.

BLAYNE. 'Thought it couldn't be worse than the Club, but I'll swear he buys ullaged liquor and doctors it with gin and ink (looking round the room.) Is this all of you to-night?

DOONE. (P.W.D.) Anthony was called out at dinner. Mingle had a pain in his tummy.

CURTISS. Miggy dies of cholera once a week in the Rains, and gets drunk on chlorodyne in between. 'Good little chap, though. Any one at the Judge's, Blayne?

BLAYNE. Cockley and his memsahib looking awfully white and fagged. Female--girl--couldn't catch the name--on her way to the Hills, under the Cockleys' charge--the Judge, and Markyn fresh from Simla--disgustingly fit.

CURTISS. Good Lord, how truly magnificent! Was there enough ice? When I mangled garbage there I got one whole lump--nearly as big as a walnut. What had Markyn to say for himself?

BLAYNE. 'Seems that every one is having a fairly good time up there in spite of the rain. By Jove, that reminds me! I know I hadn't come across just for the pleasure of your society. News! Great news! Markyn told me.

DOONE. Who's dead now?

BLAYNE. No one that I know of; but Gandy's hooked at last!

DROPPING CHORUS. How much? The Devil! Markyn was pulling your leg. Not
GANDY!

BLAYNE. (Humming.) "Yea, verily, verily, verily! Verily, verily, I say unto thee." Theodore, the gift o' God! Our Phillup! It's been given out up above.

MACKESY. (Barrister-at-Law.) Huh! Women will give out anything. What does accused say?

BLAYNE. Markyn told me that he congratulated him warily--one hand held out, t'other ready to guard. Gandy turned pink and said it was so.

CURTISS. Poor old Caddy! They all do it. Who's she? Let's hear the details.

BLAYNE. She's a girl--daughter of a Colonel Somebody.

DOONE. Simla's stiff with Colonels' daughters. Be more explicit.

BLAYNE. Wait a shake. What was her name? Thresomething. Three--

CURTISS. Stars, perhaps. Caddy knows that brand.

BLAYNE. Threegan--Minnie Threegan.

MACKESY. Threegan Isn't she a little bit of a girl with red hair?

BLAYNE. 'Bout that--from what from what Markyn said.

MACKESY. Then I've met her. She was at Lucknow last season. 'Owned a permanently juvenile Mamma, and danced damnably. I say, Jervoise, you knew the Threegans, didn't you?

JERVOISE. (Civilian of twenty-five years' service, waking up from his doze.) Eh? What's that? Knew who? How? I thought I was at Home, confound you!

MACKESY. The Threegan girl's engaged, so Blayne says.

JERVOISE. (Slowly.) Engaged--en-gaged! Bless my soul! I'm getting an old man! Little Minnie Threegan engaged. It was only the other day I went home with them in the Surat--no, the Massilia--and she was crawling about on her hands and knees among the ayahs. 'Used to call me the "Tick Tack Sahib" because I showed her my watch. And that was in Sixty--Seven-no, Seventy. Good God, how time flies! I'm an old man. I remember when Threegan married Miss Derwent--daughter of old Hooky Derwent--but that was before your time. And so the little baby's engaged to have a little baby of her own! Who's the other fool?

MACKESY. Gadsby of the Pink Hussars.

JERVOISE. 'Never met him. Threegan lived in debt, married in debt, and 'll die in debt. 'Must be glad to get the girl off his hands.

BLAYNE. Caddy has money--lucky devil. Place at Home, too.

DOONE. He comes of first-class stock. 'Can't quite understand his being caught by a Colonel's daughter, and (looking cautiously round room.) Black Infantry at that! No offence to you, Blayne.

BLAYNE. (Stiffly.) Not much, thaanks.

CURTISS. (Quoting motto of Irregular Moguls.) "We are what we are," eh, old man? But Gandy was such a superior animal as a rule. Why didn't he go Home and pick his wife there?

MACKESY. They are all alike when they come to the turn into the straight. About thirty a man begins to get sick of living alone.

CURTISS. And of the eternal muttony-chop in the morning.

DOONE. It's a dead goat as a rule, but go on, Mackesy.

MACKESY. If a man's once taken that way nothing will hold him, Do you remember Benoit of your service, Doone? They transferred him to Tharanda when his time came, and he married a platelayer's daughter, or something of that kind. She was the only female about the place.

DONE. Yes, poor brute. That smashed Benoit's chances of promotion altogether. Mrs. Benoit used to ask "Was you gem' to the dance this evenin'?"

CURTISS. Hang it all! Gandy hasn't married beneath him. There's no tarbrush in the family, I suppose.

JERVOISE. Tar-brush! Not an anna. You young fellows talk as though the man was doing the girl an honor in marrying her. You're all too conceited--nothing's good enough for you.

BLAYNE. Not even an empty Club, a dam' bad dinner at the Judge's, and a Station as sickly as a hospital. You're quite right. We're a set of Sybarites.

DOONE. Luxurious dogs, wallowing in--

CURTISS. Prickly heat between the shoulders. I'm covered with it. Let's hope Beora will be cooler.

BLAYNE. Whew! Are you ordered into camp, too? I thought the Gunners had a clean sheet.

CURTISS. No, worse luck. Two cases yesterday--one died--and if we have a third, out we go. Is there any shooting at Beora, Doone?

DOONE. The country's under water, except the patch by the Grand Trunk Road. I was there yesterday, looking at a bund, and came across four poor devils in their last stage. It's rather bad from here to Kuchara.

CURTISS. Then we're pretty certain to have a heavy go of it. Heigho! I shouldn't mind changing places with Gaddy for a while. 'Sport with Amaryllis in the shade of the Town Hall, and all that. Oh, why doesn't somebody come and marry me, instead of letting me go into cholera-camp?

MACKESY. Ask the Committee.

CURTISS. You ruffian! You'll stand me another peg for that. Blayne, what will you take? Mackesy is fine on moral grounds. Done, have you any preference?

DONE. Small glass Kummel, please. Excellent carminative, these days. Anthony told me so.

MACKESY. (Signing voucher for four drinks.) Most unfair punishment. I only thought of Curtiss as Actaeon being chivied round the billiard tables by the nymphs of Diana.

BLAYNE. Curtiss would have to import his nymphs by train. Mrs. Cockley's the only woman in the Station. She won't leave Cockley, and he's doing his best to get her to go.

CURTISS. Good, indeed! Here's Mrs. Cockley's health. To the only wife in the Station and a damned brave woman!

OMNES. (Drinking.) A damned brave woman

BLAYNE. I suppose Gandy will bring his wife here at the end of the cold weather. They are going to be married almost immediately, I believe.

CURTISS. Gandy may thank his luck that the Pink Hussars are all detachment and no headquarters this hot weather, or he'd be torn from the arms of his love as sure as death. Have you ever noticed the thorough-minded way British Cavalry take to cholera? It's because they are so expensive. If the Pinks had stood fast here, they would have been out in camp a. month ago. Yes, I should decidedly like to be Gandy.

MACKESY. He'll go Home after he's married, and send in his papers--see if he doesn't.

BLAYNE. Why shouldn't he? Hasn't he money? Would any one of us be here if we weren't paupers?

DONE. Poor old pauper! What has become of the six hundred you rooked from our table last month?

BLAYNE. It took unto itself wings. I think an enterprising tradesman got some of it, and a shroff gobbled the rest--or else I spent it.

CURTISS. Gandy never had dealings with a shroff in his life.

DONE. Virtuous Gandy! If I had three thousand a month, paid from England, I don't think I'd deal with a shroff either.

MACKESY. (Yawning.) Oh, it's a sweet life! I wonder whether matrimony would make it sweeter.

CURTISS. Ask Cockley--with his wife dying by inches!

BLAYNE. Go home and get a fool of a girl to come out to--what is it Thackeray says?-"the splendid palace of an Indian pro-consul."

DOONE. Which reminds me. My quarters leak like a sieve. I had fever last night from sleeping in a swamp. And the worst of it is, one can't do anything to a roof till the Rains are over.

CURTISS. What's wrong with you? You haven't eighty rotting Tommies to take into a running stream.

DONE. No: but I'm mixed boils and bad language. I'm a regular Job all over my body. It's sheer poverty of blood, and I don't see any chance of getting richer--either way.

BLAYNE. Can't you take leave? DONE. That's the pull you Army men have over us. Ten days are nothing in your sight. I'm so important that Government can't find a substitute if I go away. Ye-es, I'd like to be Gandy, whoever his wife may be.

CURTISS. You've passed the turn of life that Mackesy was speaking of.

DONE. Indeed I have, but I never yet had the brutality to ask a woman to share my life out here.

BLAYNE. On my soul I believe you're right. I'm thinking of Mrs. Cockley. The woman's an absolute wreck.

DONE. Exactly. Because she stays down here. The only way to keep her fit would be to send her to the Hills for eight months--and the same with any woman. I fancy I see myself taking a wife on those terms.

MACKESY. With the rupee at one and sixpence. The little Doones would be little Debra Doones, with a fine Mussoorie chi-chi anent to bring home for the holidays.

CURTISS. And a pair of be-ewtiful sambhur-horns for Done to wear, free of expense, presented by--DONE. Yes, it's an enchanting prospect. By the way, the rupee hasn't done falling yet. The time will come when we shall think ourselves lucky if we only lose half our pay.

CURTISS. Surely a third's loss enough. Who gains by the arrangement? That's what I want to know.

BLAYNE. The Silver Question! I'm going to bed if you begin squabbling Thank Goodness, here's Anthony--looking like a ghost.

Enter ANTHONY, Indian Medical Staff, very white and tired.

ANTHONY. 'Evening, Blayne. It's raining in sheets. Whiskey peg lao, khitmatgar. The roads are something ghastly.

CURTISS. How's Mingle?

ANTHONY. Very bad, and more frightened. I handed him over to Few-ton. Mingle might just as well have called him in the first place, instead of bothering me.

BLAYNE. He's a nervous little chap. What has he got, this time?

ANTHONY. 'Can't quite say. A very bad tummy and a blue funk so far. He asked me at once if it was cholera, and I told him not to be a fool. That soothed him.

CURTIS. Poor devil! The funk does half the business in a man of that build.

ANTHONY. (Lighting a cheroot.) I firmly believe the funk will kill him if he stays down. You know the amount of trouble he's been giving Fewton for the last three weeks. He's doing his very best to frighten himself into the grave.

GENERAL CHORUS. Poor little devil! Why doesn't he get away?

ANTHONY. 'Can't. He has his leave all right, but he's so dipped he can't take it, and I don't think his name on paper would raise four annas. That's in confidence, though.

MACKESY. All the Station knows it.

ANTHONY. "I suppose I shall have to die here," he said, squirming all across the bed. He's quite made up his mind to Kingdom Come. And I know he has nothing more than a wet-weather tummy if he could only keep a hand on himself.

BLAYNE. That's bad. That's very bad. Poor little Miggy. Good little chap, too. I say--

ANTHONY. What do you say?

BLAYNE. Well, look here--anyhow. If it's like that--as you say--I say fifty.

CURTISS. I say fifty.

MACKESY. I go twenty better.

DONE. Bloated Croesus of the Bar! I say fifty. Jervoise, what do you say? Hi! Wake up!

JERVOISE. Eh? What's that? What's that?

CURTISS. We want a hundred rupees from you. You're a bachelor drawing a gigantic income, and there's a man in a hole.

JERVOISE. What man? Any one dead?

BLAYNE. No, but he'll die if you don't give the hundred. Here! Here's a peg-voucher. You can see what we've signed for, and Anthony's man will come round to-morrow to collect it. So there will be no trouble.

JERVOISE. (Signing.) One hundred, E. M. J. There you are (feebly). It isn't one of your jokes, is it?

BLAYNE. No, it really is wanted. Anthony, you were the biggest poker-winner last week, and you've defrauded the tax-collector too long. Sign!

ANTHONY. Let's see. Three fifties and a seventy-two twenty-three twenty-say four hundred and twenty. That'll give him a month clear at the Hills. Many thanks, you men. I'll send round the chaprassi to-morrow.

CURTISS. You must engineer his taking the stuff, and of course you mustn't--

ANTHONY. Of course. It would never do. He'd weep with gratitude over his evening drink.

BLAYNE. That's just what he would do, damn him. Oh! I say, Anthony, you pretend to know everything. Have you heard about Gandy?

ANTHONY. No. Divorce Court at last?

BLAYNE. Worse. He's engaged!

ANTHONY. How much? He can't be!

BLAYNE. He is. He's going to be married in a few weeks. Markyn told me at the Judge's this evening. It's pukka.

ANTHONY. You don't say so? Holy Moses! There'll be a shine in the tents of Kedar.

CURTISS. 'Regiment cut up rough, think you?

ANTHONY. 'Don't know anything about the Regiment.

MACKESY. It is bigamy, then?

ANTHONY. Maybe. Do you mean to say that you men have forgotten, or is there more charity in the world than I thought?

DONE. You don't look pretty when you are trying to keep a secret. You bloat. Explain.

ANTHONY. Mrs. Herriott!

BLAYNE. (After a long pause, to the room generally.) It's my notion that we are a set of fools.

MACKESY. Nonsense. That business was knocked on the head last season. Why, young Mallard--

ANTHONY. Mallard was a candlestick, paraded as such. Think awhile. Recollect last season and the talk then. Mallard or no Mallard, did Gandy ever talk to any other woman?

CURTISS. There's something in that. It was slightly noticeable now you come to mention it. But she's at Naini Tat and he's at Simla.

ANTHONY. He had to go to Simla to look after a globe-trotter relative of his--a person with a title. Uncle or aunt.

BLAYNE And there he got engaged. No law prevents a man growing tired of a woman.

ANTHONY. Except that he mustn't do it till the woman is tired of him. And the Herriott woman was not that.

CURTISS. She may be now. Two months of Naini Tal works wonders.

DONE. Curious thing how some women carry a Fate with them. There was a Mrs. Deegie in the Central Provinces whose men invariably fell away and got married. It became a regular proverb with us when I was down there. I remember three men desperately devoted to her, and they all, one after another, took wives.

CURTISS. That's odd. Now I should have thought that Mrs. Deegie's influence would have led them to take other men's wives. It ought to have made them afraid of the judgment of Providence.

ANTHONY. Mrs. Herriott will make Gandy afraid of something more than the
judgment of Providence, I fancy.

BLAYNE. Supposing things are as you say, he'll be a fool to face her. He'll sit tight at Simla.

ANTHONY. 'Shouldn't be a bit surprised if he went off to Naini to explain. He's an unaccountable sort of man, and she's likely to be a more than unaccountable woman.

DONE. What makes you take her character away so confidently?

ANTHONY. Primum tern pus. Caddy was her first and a woman doesn't al-low
her first man to drop away without expostulation. She justifies the first transfer of affection to herself by swearing that it is forever and ever. Consequently--

BLAYNE. Consequently, we are sitting here till past one o'clock, talking scandal like a set of Station cats. Anthony, it's all your fault. We were perfectly respectable till you came in Go to bed. I'm off, Good-night all.

CURTISS. Past one! It's past two by Jove, and here's the khit coming for the late charge. Just Heavens! One, two, three, four, five rupees to pay for the pleasure of saying that a poor little beast of a woman is no better than she should be. I'm ashamed of myself. Go to bed, you slanderous villains, and if I'm sent to Beora to-morrow, be prepared to hear I'm dead before paying my card account!

THE TENTS OF KEDAR

Only why should it be with pain at all Why must I 'twix the leaves of corona! Put any kiss of pardon on thy brow? Why should the other women know so much, And talk together--Such the look and such The smile he used to love with, then as now.--Any Wife to any Husband.

SCENE--A Naini Tal dinner for thirty-four. Plate, wines, crockery, and khitmatgars carefully calculated to scale of Rs. 6000 per mensem, less Exchange. Table split lengthways by bank of flowers.

MRS. HERRIOTT. (After conversation has risen to proper pitch.) Ah! 'Didn't see you in the crush in the drawing-room. (Sotto voce.) Where have you been all this while, Pip?

CAPTAIN GADSBY. (Turning from regularly ordained dinner partner and settling hock glasses.) Good evening. (Sotto voce.) Not quite so loud another time. You've no notion how your voice carries. (Aside.) So much for shirking the written explanation. It'll have to be a verbal one now. Sweet prospect! How on earth am I to tell her that I am a respectable, engaged member of society and it's all over between us?

MRS. H. I've a heavy score against you. Where were you at the Monday Pop? Where were you on Tuesday? Where were you at the Lamonts' tennis? I was looking everywhere.

CAPT. G. For me! Oh, I was alive somewhere, I suppose. (Aside.) It's for Minnie's sake, but it's going to be dashed unpleasant.

MRS. H. Have I done anything to offend you? I never meant it if I have. I couldn't help going for a ride with the Vaynor man. It was promised a week before you came up.

CAPT. G. I didn't know--

MRS. H. It really was.

CAPT. G. Anything about it, I mean.

MRS. H. What has upset you today? All these days? You haven't been near me for four whole days--nearly one hundred hours. Was it kind of you, Pip? And I've been looking forward so much to your coming.

CAPT. G. Have you?

MRS. H. You know I have! I've been as foolish as a schoolgirl about it. I made a little calendar and put it in my card-case, and every time the twelve o'clock gun went off I scratched out a square and said: "That brings me nearer to Pip. My Pip!"

CAPT. G. (With an uneasy laugh). What will Mackler think if you neglect him so?

MRS. H. And it hasn't brought you nearer. You seem farther away than ever. Are you sulking about something? I know your temper.

CAPT. G. No.

MRS. H. Have I grown old in' the last few months, then? (Reaches forward to bank of flowers for menu-card.)

PARTNER ON LEFT. Allow me. (Hands menu-card. MRS. H. keeps her arm at
full stretch for three seconds.)

MRS. H. (To partner.) Oh, thanks. I didn't see. (Turns right again.) Is anything in me changed at all?

CAPT. G. For Goodness's sake go on with your dinner! You must eat something. Try one of those cutlet arrangements. (Aside.) And I fancied she had good shoulders, once upon a time! What an ass a man can make of himself!

MRS. H. (Helping herself to a paper frill, seven peas, some stamped carrots and a spoonful of gravy.) That isn't an answer. Tell me whether I have done anything.

CAPT. G. (Aside.) If it isn't ended here there will be a ghastly scene somewhere else. If only I'd written to her and stood the racket--at long range! (To Khitmatgar.) Han! Simpkin do. (Aloud.) I'll tell you later on.

MRS. H. Tell me now. It must be some foolish misunderstanding, and you know that there was to be nothing of that sort between us. We, of all people in the world, can't afford it. Is it the Vaynor man, and don't you like to say so? On my honor--

CAPT. G. I haven't given the Vaynor man a thought.

MRS. H. But how d'you know that I haven't?

CAPT. G. (Aside.) Here's my chance and may the Devil help me through with it. (Aloud and measuredly.) Believe me, I do not care how often or how tenderly you think of the Vaynor man.

MRS. H. I wonder if you mean that! Oh, what is the good of squabbling and pretending to misunderstand when you are only up for so short a time? Pip, don't be a stupid!

Follows a pause, during which he crosses his left leg over his right and continues his dinner.

CAPT. G. (In answer to the thunderstorm in her eyes.) Corns--my worst.

MRS. H. Upon my word, you are the very rudest man in the world! I'll never do it again.

CAPT. G. (Aside.) No, I don't think you will; but I wonder what you will do before it's all over. (To Khitmatgar.) Thorah ur Simpkin do.

MRS. H. Well! Haven't you the grace to apologize, bad man?

CAPT. G. (Aside.) I mustn't let it drift back now. Trust a woman for being as blind as a bat when she won't see.

MRS. H. I'm waiting; or would you like me to dictate a form of apology?

CAPT. G. (Desperately.) By all means dictate.

MRS. H. (Lightly.) Very well. Rehearse your several Christian names after me and go on: "Profess my sincere repentance."

CAPT. G. "Sincere repentance."

MRS. H. "For having behaved"--

CAPT. G. (Aside.) At last! I wish to Goodness she'd look away. "For having behaved"--as I have behaved, and declare that I am thoroughly and heartily sick of the whole business, and take this opportunity of making clear my intention of ending it, now, henceforward, and forever. (Aside.) If any one had told me I should be such a blackguard--!

MRS. H. (Shaking a spoonful of potato chips into her plate.) That's not a pretty joke.

CAPT. G. No. It's a reality. (Aside.) I wonder if smashes of this kind are always so raw.

MRS. H. Really, Pip, you're getting more absurd every day.

CAPT. G. I don't think you quite understand me. Shall I repeat it?

MRS. H. No! For pity's sake don't do that. It's too terrible, even in fur.

CAPT. G. I'll let her think it over for a while. But I ought to be horsewhipped.

MRS. H. I want to know what you meant by what you said just now.

CAPT. G. Exactly what I said. No less.

MRS. H. But what have I done to deserve it? What have I done?

CAPT. G. (Aside.) If she only wouldn't look at me. (Aloud and very slowly, his eyes on his plate.) D'you remember that evening in July, before the Rains broke, when you said that the end would have to come sooner or later--and you wondered for which of US it would come first?

MRS. H. Yes! I was only joking. And you swore that, as long as there was breath in your body, it should never come. And I believed you.

CAPT. G. (Fingering menu-card.) Well, it has. That's all.

A long pause, during which MRS. H. bows her head and rolls the bread-twist into little pellets; G. stares at the oleanders.

MRS. H. (Throwing back her head and laughing naturally.) They train us women well, don't they, Pip?

CAPT. G. (Brutally, touching shirt-stud.) So far as the expression goes. (Aside.) It isn't in her nature to take things quietly. There'll be an explosion yet.

MRS. H. (With a shudder.) Thank you. B-but even Red Indians allow people to wriggle when they're being tortured, I believe. (Slips fan from girdle and fans slowly: rim of fan level with chin.)

PARTNER ON LEFT. Very close tonight, isn't it? 'You find it too much for you?

MRS. H. Oh, no, not in the least. But they really ought to have punkahs, even in your cool Naini Tal, oughtn't they? (Turns, dropping fan and raising eyebrows.)

CAPT. G. It's all right. (Aside.) Here comes the storm!

MRS. H. (Her eyes on the tablecloth: fan ready in right hand.) It was very cleverly managed, Pip, and I congratulate you. You swore--you never contented yourself with merely Saying a thing--you swore that, as far as lay in your power, you'd make my wretched life pleasant for me. And you've denied me the consolation of breaking down. I should have done it--indeed I should. A woman would hardly have thought of this refinement, my kind, considerate friend. (Fan-guard as before.) You have explained things so tenderly and truthfully, too! You haven't spoken or written a word of warning, and you have let me believe in you till the last minute. You haven't condescended to give me your reason yet. No! A woman could not have managed it half so well. Are there many men like you in the world?

CAPT. G. I'm sure I don't know. (To Khitmatgar.) Ohe! Simpkin do.

MRS. H. You call yourself a man of the world, don't you? Do men of the world behave like Devils when they a woman the honor to get tired of her?

CAPT. G. I'm sure I don't know. Don't speak so loud!

MRS. H. Keep us respectable, O Lord, whatever happens. Don't be afraid of my compromising you. You've chosen your ground far too well, and I've been properly brought up. (Lowering fan.) Haven't you any pity, Pip, except for yourself?

CAPT. G. Wouldn't it be rather impertinent of me to say that I'm sorry for you?

MRS. H. I think you have said it once or twice before. You're growing very careful of my feelings. My God, Pip, I was a good woman once! You said I was. You've made me what I am. What are you going to do with me? What are you going to do with me? Won't you say that you are sorry? (Helps herself to iced asparagus.)

CAPT. G. I am sorry for you, if you Want the pity of such a brute as I am. I'm awf'ly sorry for you.

MRS. H. Rather tame for a man of the world. Do you think that that admission clears you?

CAPT. G. What can I do? I can only tell you what I think of myself. You can't think worse than that?

MRS. H. Oh, yes, I can! And now, will you tell me the reason of all this? Remorse? Has Bayard been suddenly conscience-stricken?

CAPT. G. (Angrily, his eyes still lowered.) No! The thing has come to an end on my side. That's all. Mafisch!

MRS. H. "That's all. Mafisch!" As though I were a Cairene Dragoman. You used to make prettier speeches. D'you remember when you said?--

CAPT. G. For Heaven's sake don't bring that back! Call me anything you like and I'll admit it--

MRS. H. But you don't care to be reminded of old lies? If I could hope to hurt you one-tenth as much as you have hurt me to-night--No, I wouldn't--I couldn't do it--liar though you are.

CAPT. G. I've spoken the truth.

MRS. H. My dear Sir, you flatter yourself. You have lied over the reason. Pip, remember that I know you as you don't know yourself. You have been everything to me, though you are--(Fan-guard.) Oh, what a contemptible Thing it is! And so you are merely tired of me?

CAPT. G. Since you insist upon my repeating it--Yes.

MRS. H. Lie the first. I wish I knew a coarser word. Lie seems so in-effectual in your case. The fire has just died out and there is no fresh one? Think for a minute, Pip, if you care whether I despise you more than I do. Simply Mafisch, is it?

CAPT. G. Yes. (Aside.) I think I deserve this.

MRS. H. Lie number two. Before the next glass chokes you, tell me her name.

CAPT. G. (Aside.) I'll make her pay for dragging Minnie into the business! (Aloud.) Is it likely?

MRS. H. Very likely if you thought that it would flatter your vanity. You'd cry my name on the house-tops to make people turn round.

CAPT. G. I wish I had. There would have been an end to this business.

MRS. H. Oh, no, there would not--And so you were going to be virtuous and blase', were you? To come to me and say: "I've done with you. The incident is clo-osed." I ought to be proud of having kept such a man so long.

CAPT. G. (Aside.) It only remains to pray for the end of the dinner. (Aloud.) You know what I think of myself.

MRS. H. As it's the only person in he world you ever do think of, and as I know your mind thoroughly, I do. You want to get it all over and--Oh, I can't keep you back! And you're going--think of it, Pip--to throw me over for another woman. And you swore that all other women were--Pip, my Pip! She can't care for you as I do. Believe me, she can't. Is it any one that I know?

CAPT. G. Thank Goodness it isn't. (Aside.) I expected a cyclone, but not an earthquake.

MRS. H. She can't! Is there anything that I wouldn't do for you--or haven't done? And to think that I should take this trouble over you, knowing what you are! Do you despise me for it?

CAPT. G. (Wiping his mouth to hide a smile.) Again? It's entirely a work of charity on your part.

MRS. H. Ahhh! But I have no right to resent it.--Is she better-looking than I? Who was it said?--

CAPT. G. No--not that!

MRS. H. I'll be more merciful than you were. Don't you know that all women are alike?

CAPT. G. (Aside.) Then this is the exception that proves the rule.

MRS. H. All of them! I'll tell you anything you like. I will, upon my word! They only want the admiration--from anybody--no matter who--anybody! But there is always one man that they care for more than any one else in the world, and would sacrifice all the others to. Oh, do listen! I've kept the Vaynor man trotting after me like a poodle, and he believes that he is the only man I am interested in. I'll tell you what he said to me.

CAPT. G. Spare him. (Aside.) I wonder what his version is.

MRS. H. He's been waiting for me to look at him all through dinner. Shall I do it, and you can see what an idiot he looks?

CAPT. G. "But what imports the nomination of this gentleman?"

MRS. H. Watch! (Sends a glance to the Vaynor man, who tries vainly to combine a mouthful of ice pudding, a smirk of self-satisfaction, a glare of intense devotion, and the stolidity of a British dining countenance.)

CAPT. G. (Critically.) He doesn't look pretty. Why didn't you wait till the spoon was out of his mouth?

MRS. H. To amuse you. She'll make an exhibition of you as I've made of him; and people will laugh at you. Oh, Pip, can't you see that? It's as plain as the noonday Sun. You'll be trotted about and told lies, and made a fool of like the others. I never made a fool of you, did I?

CAPT. G. (Aside.) What a clever little woman it is!

MRS. H. Well, what have you to say?

CAPT. G. I feel better.

MRS. H. Yes, I suppose so, after I have come down to your level. I couldn't have done it if I hadn't cared for you so much. I have spoken the truth.

CAPT. G. It doesn't alter the situation.

MRS. H. (Passionately.) Then she has said that she cares for you! Don't believe her, Pip. It's a lie--as bad as yours to me!

CAPT. G. Ssssteady! I've a notion that a friend of yours is looking at you.

MRS. H. He! I hate him. He introduced you to me.

CAPT. G. (Aside.) And some people would like women to assist in making the laws. Introduction to imply condonement. (Aloud.) Well, you see, if you can remember so far back as that, I couldn't, in' common politeness, refuse the offer.

MRS. H. In common politeness I We have got beyond that!

CAPT. G. (Aside.) Old ground means fresh trouble. (Aloud.) On my honor

MRS. H. Your what? Ha, ha!

CAPT. G. Dishonor, then. She's not what you imagine. I meant to--

MRS. H. Don't tell me anything about her! She won't care for you, and when you come back, after having made an exhibition of yourself, you'll find me occupied with--

CAPT. G. (Insolently.) You couldn't while I am alive. (Aside.) If that doesn't bring her pride to her rescue, nothing will.

MRS. H. (Drawing herself up.) Couldn't do it? I' (Softening.) You're right. I don't believe I could--though you are what you are--a coward and a liar in grain.

CAPT. G. It doesn't hurt so much after your little lecture--with demonstrations.

MRS. H. One mass of vanity! Will nothing ever touch you in this life? There must be a Hereafter if it's only for the benefit of--But you will have it all to yourself.

CAPT. G. (Under his eyebrows.) Are you certain of that?

MRS. H. I shall have had mine in this life; and it will serve me right.

CAPT. G. But the admiration that you insisted on so strongly a moment ago? (Aside.) Oh, I am a brute!

MRS. H. (Fiercely.) Will that con-sole me for knowing that you will go to her with the same words, the same arguments, and the--the same pet names you used to me? And if she cares for you, you two will laugh over my story. Won't that be punishment heavy enough even for me--even for me?--And it's all useless. That's another punishment.

CAPT. G. (Feebly.) Oh, come! I'm not so low as you think.

MRS. H. Not now, perhaps, but you will be. Oh, Pip, if a woman flatters your vanity, there's nothing on earth that you would not tell her; and no meanness that you would not do. Have I known you so long without knowing that?

CAPT. G. If you can trust me in nothing else--and I don't see why I should be trusted--you can count upon my holding my tongue.

MRS. H. If you denied everything you've said this evening and declared it was all in' fun (a long pause), I'd trust you. Not otherwise. All I ask is, don't tell her my name. Please don't. A man might forget: a woman never would. (Looks up table and sees hostess beginning to collect eyes.) So it's all ended, through no fault of mine--Haven't I behaved beautifully? I've accepted your dismissal, and you managed it as cruelly as you could, and I have made you respect my sex, haven't I? (Arranging gloves and fan.) I only pray that she'll know you some day as I know you now. I wouldn't be you then, for I think even your conceit will be hurt. I hope she'll pay you back the humiliation you've brought on me. I hope--No. I don't! I can't give you up! I must have something to look forward to or I shall go crazy. When it's all over, come back to me, come back to me, and you'll find that you're my Pip still!

CAPT. G. (Very clearly.) False move, and you pay for it. It's a girl!

MRS. H. (Rising.) Then it was true! They said--but I wouldn't insult you by asking. A girl! I was a girl not very long ago. Be good to her, Pip. I daresay she believes in' you.

Goes out with an uncertain smile. He watches her through the door, and settles into a chair as the men redistribute themselves.

CAPT. G. Now, if there is any Power who looks after this world, will He kindly tell me what I have done? (Reaching out for the claret, and half aloud.) What have I done?

WITH ANY AMAZEMENT

And are not afraid with any amazement.--Marriage Service.

SCENE.--A bachelor's bedroom-toilet-table arranged with unnatural neatness. CAPTAIN GADSBY asleep and snoring heavily. Time, 10:30 A. M.--a glorious autumn day at Simla. Enter delicately Captain MAFFLIN of GADSBY's regiment. Looks at sleeper, and shakes his head murmuring "Poor Gaddy." Performs violent fantasia with hair-brushes on chairback.

CAPT. M. Wake up, my sleeping beauty! (Roars.)

"Uprouse ye, then, my merry merry men! It is our opening day! It is our opening da-ay!"

Gaddy, the little dicky-birds have been billing and cooing for ever so long; and I'm here!

CAPT. G. (Sitting up and yawning.) 'Mornin'. This is awf'ly good of you, old fellow. Most awf'ly good of you. 'Don't know what I should do without you. 'Pon my soul, I don't. 'Haven't slept a wink all night.

CAPT. M. I didn't get in till half-past eleven. 'Had a look at you then, and you seemed to be sleeping as soundly as a condemned criminal.

CAPT. G. Jack, if you want to make those disgustingly worn-out jokes, you'd better go away. (With portentous gravity.) It's the happiest day in my life.

CAPT. M. (Chuckling grimly.) Not by a very long chalk, my son. You're going through some of the most refined torture you've ever known. But be calm. I am with you. 'Shun! Dress!

CAPT. G. Eh! Wha-at?

CAPT. M. Do you suppose that you are your own master for the next twelve hours? If you do, of course-(Makes for the door.)

CAPT. G. No! For Goodness' sake, old man, don't do that! You'll see through, won't you? I've been mugging up that beastly drill, and can't remember a line of it.

CAPT. M. (Overturning G.'s uniform.) Go and tub. Don't bother me. I'll give you ten minutes to dress in.

(Interval, filled by the noise as of one splashing in the bath-room.)

CAPT. G. (Emerging from dressing-room.) What time is it?

CAPT. M. Nearly eleven.

CAPT. G. Five hours more. O Lord!

CAPT. M. (Aside.) 'First sign of funk, that. 'Wonder if it's going to spread. (Aloud.) Come along to breakfast.

CAPT. G. I can't eat anything. I don't want any breakfast.

CAPT. M. (Aside.) So early! (Aloud) CAPTAIN Gadsby, I order you to eat breakfast, and a dashed good breakfast, too. None of your bridal airs and graces with me!

Leads G. downstairs and stands over him while he eats two chops.

CAPT. G. (Who has looked at his watch thrice in the last five minutes.) What time is it?

CAPT. M. Time to come for a walk. Light up.

CAPT. G. I haven't smoked for ten days, and I won't now. (Takes cheroot which M. has cut for him, and blows smoke through his nose luxuriously.) We aren't going down the Mall, are we?

CAPT. M. (Aside.) They're all alike in these stages. (Aloud.) No, my Vestal. We're going along the quietest road we can find.

CAPT. G. Any chance of seeing Her? CAPT. M. Innocent! No! Come along, and, if you want me for the final obsequies, don't cut my eye out with your stick.

CAPT. G. (Spinning round.) I say, isn't She the dearest creature that ever walked? What's the time? What comes after "wilt thou take this woman"?

CAPT. M. You go for the ring. R'clect it'll be on the top of my right-hand little finger, and just be careful how you draw it off, because I shall have the Verger's fees somewhere in my glove.

CAPT. G. (Walking forward hastily.) D---- the Verger! Come along! It's past twelve and I haven't seen Her since yesterday evening. (Spinning round again.) She's an absolute angel, Jack, and She's a dashed deal too good for me. Look here, does She come up the aisle on my arm, or how?

CAPT. M. If I thought that there was the least chance of your remembering anything for two consecutive minutes, I'd tell you. Stop passaging about like that!

CAPT. G. (Halting in the middle of the road.) I say, Jack.

CAPT. M. Keep quiet for another ten minutes if you can, you lunatic; and walk!

The two tramp at five miles an hour for fifteen minutes.

CAPT. G. What's the time? How about the cursed wedding-cake and the slippers? They don't throw 'em about in church, do they?

CAPT. M. In-variably. The Padre leads off with his boots.

CAPT. G. Confound your silly soul! Don't make fun of me. I can't stand it, and I won't!

CAPT. M. (Untroubled.) So-ooo, old horse You'll have to sleep for a couple of hours this afternoon.

CAPT. G. (Spinning round.) I'm not going to be treated like a dashed child. Understand that!

CAPT. M. (Aside.) Nerves gone to fiddle-strings. What a day we're having! (Tenderly putting his hand on G.'s shoulder.) My David, how long have you known this Jonathan? Would I come up here to make a fool of you--after all these years?

CAPT. G. (Penitently.) I know, I know, Jack--but I'm as upset as I can be. Don't mind what I say. Just hear me run through the drill and see if I've got it all right:-"To have and to hold for better or worse, as it was in the beginning, is now, and ever shall be, world without end, so help me God. Amen."

CAPT. M. (Suffocating with suppressed laughter.) Yes. That's about the gist of it. I'll prompt if you get into a hat.

CAPT. G. (Earnestly.) Yes, you'll stick by me, Jack, won't you? I'm awfully happy, but I don't mind telling you that I'm in a blue funk!

CAPT. M. (Gravely.) Are you? I should never have noticed it. You don't look like it.

CAPT. G. Don't I? That's all right. (Spinning round.) On my soul and honor, Jack, She's the sweetest little angel that ever came down from the sky. There isn't a woman on earth fit to speak to Her.

CAPT. M. (Aside.) And this is old Gandy! (Aloud.) Go on if it relieves you.

CAPT. G. You can laugh! That's all you wild asses of bachelors are fit for.

CAPT. M. (Drawling.) You never would wait for the troop to come up. You aren't quite married yet, y'know.

CAPT. G. Ugh! That reminds me. I don't believe I shall be able to get into any boots Let's go home and try 'em on (Hurries forward.)

CAPT. M. 'Wouldn't be in your shoes for anything that Asia has to offer.

CAPT. G. (Spinning round.) That just shows your hideous blackness of soul--your dense stupidity--your brutal narrow-mindedness. There's only one fault about you. You're the best of good fellows, and I don't know what I should have done without you, but--you aren't married. (Wags his head gravely.) Take a wife, Jack.

CAPT. M. (With a face like a wall.) Va-as. Whose for choice?

CAPT. G. If you're going to be a blackguard, I'm going on--What's the time?

CAPT. M. (Hums.)--

"An' since 'twas very clear we drank only ginger-beer,
   Faith, there must ha' been some stingo in the ginger."

Come back, you maniac. I'm going to take you home, and you're going to lie down.

CAPT. G. What on earth do I want to lie down for?

CAPT. M. Give me a light from your cheroot and see.

CAPT. G. (Watching cheroot-butt quiver like a tuning-fork.) Sweet state I'm in!

CAPT. M. You are. I'll get you a peg and you'll go to sleep.

They return and M. compounds a four-finger peg.

CAPT. G. O bus! bus! It'll make me as drunk as an owl.

CAPT. M. 'Curious thing, 'twon't have the slightest effect on you. Drink it off, chuck yourself down there, and go to bye-bye.

CAPT. G. It's absurd. I sha'n't sleep, I know I sha'n't!

(Falls into heavy doze at end of seven minutes. CAPT. M. watches him tenderly.)

CAPT. M. Poor old Gandy! I've seen a few turned off before, but never one who went to the gallows in this condition. 'Can't tell how it affects 'em, though. It's the thoroughbreds that sweat when they're backed into double-harness.--And that's the man who went through the guns at Amdheran like a devil possessed of devils. (Leans over G.) But this is worse than the guns, old pal--worse than the guns, isn't it? (G. turns in his sleep, and M. touches him clumsily on the forehead.) Poor, dear old Gaddy I Going like the rest of 'em--going like the rest of 'em--Friend that sticketh closer than a brother--eight years. Dashed bit of a slip of a girl--eight weeks! And--where's your friend? (Smokes disconsolately till church clock strikes three.)

CAPT. M. Up with you! Get into your kit.

CAPT. C. Already? Isn't it too soon? Hadn't I better have a shave?

CAPT. M. No! You're all right. (Aside.) He'd chip his chin to pieces.

CAPT. C. What's the hurry?

CAPT. M. You've got to be there first.

CAPT. C. To be stared at?

CAPT. M. Exactly. You're part of the show. Where's the burnisher? Your spurs are in a shameful state.

CAPT. G. (Gruffly.) Jack, I be damned if you shall do that for me.

CAPT. M. (More gruffly.) Dry' up and get dressed! If I choose to clean your spurs, you're under my orders.

CAPT. G. dresses. M. follows suit.

CAPT. M. (Critically, walking round.) M'yes, you'll do. Only don't look so like a criminal. Ring, gloves, fees--that's all right for me. Let your moustache alone. Now, if the ponies are ready, we'll go.

CAPT. G. (Nervously.) It's much too soon. Let's light up! Let's have a peg! Let's--CAPT. M. Let's make bally asses of ourselves!

BELLS. (Without.)--

"Good-peo-ple-all To prayers-we call."

CAPT. M. There go the bells! Come an--unless you'd rather not. (They ride off.)

BELLS.--

"We honor the King And Brides joy do bring--Good tidings we tell, And ring the Dead's knell."

CAPT. G. (Dismounting at the door of the Church.) I say, aren't we much too soon? There are no end of people inside. I say, aren't we much too late? Stick by me, Jack! What the devil do I do?

CAPT. M. Strike an attitude at the head of the aisle and wait for Her. (G. groans as M. wheels him into position before three hundred eyes.)

CAPT. M. (Imploringly.) Gaddy, if you love me, for pity's sake, for the Honor of the Regiment, stand up! Chuck yourself into your uniform! Look like a man! I've got to speak to the Padre a minute. (G. breaks into

a gentle Perspiration.) your face I'll never man again. Stand up!
(Visibly.) If you wipe your face I'll never be your best man again. Stand
up! (G. Trembles visibly.)

CAPT. M. (Returning.) She's coming now. Look out when the music starts.
There's the organ beginning to clack.

(Bride steps out of 'rickshaw at Church door. G. catches a glimpse of her
and takes heart.)

ORGAN.--

"The Voice that breathed o'er Eden,
That earliest marriage day,
The primal marriage-blessing,
It hath not passed away."

CAPT. M. (Watching G.) By Jove! He is looking well. 'Didn't think he had
it in him.

CAPT. G. How long does this hymn go on for?

CAPT. M. It will be over directly. (Anxiously.) Beginning to beltch and
gulp. Hold on, Gabby, and think o' the Regiment.

CAPT. G. (Measuredly.) I say there's a big brown lizard crawling up that
wall.

CAPT. M. My Sainted Mother! The last stage of collapse!

Bride comes Up to left of altar, lifts her eyes once to G., who is
suddenly smitten mad.

CAPT. G. (TO himself again and again.) Little Featherweight's a woman--a woman! And I thought she was a little girl.

CAPT. M. (In a whisper.) Form the halt--inward wheel.

CAPT. G. obeys mechanically and the ceremony proceeds.

PADRE.... only unto her as ye both shall live?

CAPT. G. (His throat useless.) Ha--hmmm!

CAPT. M. Say you will or you won't. There's no second deal here.

Bride gives response with perfect calmness, and is given away by the father.

CAPT. G. (Thinking to show his learning.) Jack give me away now, quick!

CAPT. M. You've given yourself away quite enough. Her right hand, man! Repeat! Repeat! "Theodore Philip." Have you forgotten your own name?

CAPT. G. stumbles through Affirmation, which Bride repeats without a tremor.

CAPT. M. Now the ring! Follow the Padre! Don't pull off my glove! Here it is! Great Cupid, he's found his voice.

CAPT. G. repeats Troth in a voice to be heard to the end of the Church and turns on his heel.

CAPT. M. (Desperately.) Rein back! Back to your troop! 'Tisn't half legal yet.

PADRE.... joined together let no man put asunder.

CAPT. G. paralyzed with fear jibs after Blessing.

CAPT. M. (Quickly.) On your own front--one length. Take her with you. I don't come. You've nothing to say. (CAPT. G. jingles up to altar.)

CAPT. M. (In a piercing rattle meant to be a whisper.) Kneel, you stiff-necked ruffian! Kneel!

PADRE... whose daughters are ye so long as ye do well and are not afraid with any amazement.

CAPT. M. Dismiss! Break off! Left wheel!

All troop to vestry. They sign.

CAPT. M. Kiss Her, Gaddy.

CAPT. G. (Rubbing the ink into his glove.) Eh! Wha-at?

CAPT. M. (Taking one pace to Bride.) If you don't, I shall.

CAPT. G. (Interposing an arm.) Not this journey!

General kissing, in which CAPT. G. is pursued by unknown female.

CAPT. G. (Faintly to M.) This is Hades! Can I wipe my face now?

CAPT. M. My responsibility has ended. Better ask Misses GADSBY.

CAPT. G. winces as though shot and procession is Mendelssohned out of Church to house, where usual tortures take place over the wedding-cake.

CAPT. M. (At table.) Up with you, Gaddy. They expect a speech.

CAPT. G. (After three minutes' agony.) Ha-hmmm. (Thunders Of applause.)

CAPT. M. Doocid good, for a first attempt. Now go and change your kit while Mamma is weeping over "the Missus." (CAPT. G. disappears. CAPT. M. starts up tearing his hair.) It's not half legal. Where are the shoes? Get an ayah.

AYAH. Missie Captain Sahib done gone band karo all the jutis.

CAPT. M. (Brandishing scab larded sword.) Woman, produce those shoes Some one lend me a bread-knife. We mustn't crack Gaddy's head more than it is. (Slices heel off white satin slipper and puts slipper up his sleeve.)

Where is the Bride? (To the company at large.) Be tender with that rice. It's a heathen custom. Give me the big bag.

* * * * * *

Bride slips out quietly into 'rickshaw and departs toward the sunset.

CAPT. M. (In the open.) Stole away, by Jove! So much the worse for Gaddy! Here he is. Now Gaddy, this'll be livelier than Amdberan! Where's your horse?

CAPT. G. (Furiously, seeing that the women are out of an earshot.) Where the--is my Wife?

CAPT. M. Half-way to Mahasu by this time. You'll have to ride like Young Lochinvar.

Horse comes round on his hind legs; refuses to let G. handle him.

CAPT. G. Oh you will, will you? Get 'round, you brute--you hog--you beast! Get round!

Wrenches horse's head over, nearly breaking lower jaw: swings himself into saddle, and sends home both spurs in the midst of a spattering gale of Best Patna.

CAPT. M. For your life and your love-ride, Gaddy--And God bless you!

Throws half a pound of rice at G. who disappears, bowed forward on the saddle, in a cloud of sunlit dust.

CAPT. M. I've lost old Gaddy. (Lights cigarette and strolls off, singing absently):--

"You may carve it on his tombstone, you may cut it on his card, That a young man married is a young man marred!"

Miss DEERCOURT. (From her horse.) Really, Captain Mafflin! You are more plain spoken than polite!

CAPT. M. (Aside.) They say marriage is like cholera. 'Wonder who'll be the next victim.

White satin slipper slides from his sleeve and falls at his feet. Left wondering.

THE GARDEN OF EDEN And ye shall be as--Gods!

SCENE.--Thymy grass-plot at back of t!'e Mahasu dak-bungalow,
overlooking little wooded valley. On the left, glimpse of the Dead
Forest of Fagoo; on the right, Simla Hills. In background, line of the
Snows. CAPTAIN GADSBY, now three weeks a husband, is smoking the pipe of
peace on a rug in the sunshine. Banjo and tobacco-pouch on rug. Overhead
the Fagoo eagles. MRS. G. comes out of bungalow.

MRS. G. My husband! CAPT. G. (Lazily, with intense enjoyment.) Eh,
wha-at? Say that again.

MRS. G. I've written to Mamma and told her that we shall be back on the
17th.

CAPT. G. Did you give her my love?

MRS. G. No, I kept all that for myself. (Sitting down by his side.) I
thought you wouldn't mind.

CAPT. G. (With mock sternness.) I object awf'ly. How did you know that
it was yours to keep?

MRS. G. I guessed, Phil.

CAPT. G. (Rapturously.) Lit-tle Featherweight!

MRS. G. I won' t be called those sporting pet names, bad boy.

CAPT. G. You'll be called anything I choose. Has it ever occurred to you, Madam, that you are my Wife?

MRS. G. It has. I haven't ceased wondering at it yet.

CAPT. G. Nor I. It seems so strange; and yet, somehow, it doesn't. (Confidently.) You see, it could have been no one else.

MRS. G. (Softly.) No. No one else--for me or for you. It must have been all arranged from the beginning. Phil, tell me again what made you care for me.

CAPT. G. How could I help it? You were you, you know.

MRS. G. Did you ever want to help it? Speak the truth!

CAPT. G. (A twinkle in his eye.) I did, darling, just at the first. Rut only at the very first. (Chuckles.) I called you--stoop low and I'll whisper--"a little beast." Ho! Ho! Ho!

MRS. G. (Taking him by the moustache and making him sit up.) "A--little--beast!" Stop laughing over your crime! And yet you had the--the--awful cheek to propose to me!

CAPT. C. I'd changed my mind then. And you weren't a little beast any more.

MRS. G. Thank you, sir! And when was I ever?

CAPT. G. Never! But that first day, when you gave me tea in that peach-colored muslin gown thing, you looked--you did indeed, dear--such an absurd little mite. And I didn't know what to say to you.

MRS. G. (Twisting moustache.) So you said "little beast." Upon my word, Sir! I called you a "Crrrreature," but I wish now I had called you something worse.

CAPT. G. (Very meekly.) I apologize, but you're hurting me awf'ly. (Interlude.) You're welcome to torture me again on those terms.

MRS. G. Oh, why did you let me do it?

CAPT. G. (Looking across valley.) No reason in particular, but--if it amused you or did you any good--you might--wipe those dear little boots of yours on me.

MRS. G. (Stretching out her hands.) Don't! Oh, don't! Philip, my King, please don't talk like that. It's how I feel. You're so much too good for me. So much too good!

CAPT. G. Me! I'm not fit to put my arm around you. (Puts it round.)

MRS. C. Yes, you are. But I--what have I ever done?

CAPT. G. Given me a wee bit of your heart, haven't you, my Queen!

MRS. G. That's nothing. Any one would do that. They cou-couldn't help it.

CAPT. G. Pussy, you'll make me horribly conceited. Just when I was beginning to feel so humble, too.

MRS. G. Humble! I don't believe it's in your character.

CAPT. G. What do you know of my character, Impertinence?

MRS. G. Ah, but I shall, shan't I, Phil? I shall have time in all the years and years to come, to know everything about you; and there will be no secrets between us.

CAPT. G. Little witch! I believe you know me thoroughly already.

MRS. G. I think I can guess. You're selfish?

CAPT. G. Yes.

MRS. G. Foolish?

CAPT. G. Very.

MRS. G. And a dear?

CAPT. G. That is as my lady pleases.

MRS. G. Then your lady is pleased. (A pause.) D'you know that we're two solemn, serious, grown-up people--CAPT. G. (Tilting her straw hat over her eyes.) You grown-up! Pooh! You're a baby.

MRS. G. And we're talking nonsense.

CAPT. G. Then let's go on talking nonsense. I rather like it. Pussy, I'll tell you a secret. Promise not to repeat?

MRS. G. Ye-es. Only to you.

CAPT. G. I love you.

MRS. G. Re-ally! For how long?

CAPT. G. Forever and ever.

MRS. G. That's a long time.

CAPT. G. 'Think so? It's the shortest I can do with.

MRS. G. You're getting quite clever.

CAPT. G. I'm talking to you.

MRS. G. Prettily turned. Hold up your stupid old head and I'll pay you for it.

CAPT. G. (Affecting supreme contempt.) Take it yourself if you want it.

MRS. G. I've a great mind to--and I will! (Takes it and is repaid with interest.)

CAPT. G, Little Featherweight, it's my opinion that we are a couple of idiots.

MRS. G. We're the only two sensible people in the world. Ask the eagle. He's coming by.

CAPT. G. Ah! I dare say he's seen a good many sensible people at Mahasu. They say that those birds live for ever so long.

MRS. G. How long?

CAPT. G. A hundred and twenty years.

MRS. G. A hundred and twenty years! O-oh! And in a hundred and twenty years where will these two sensible people be?

CAPT. G. What does it matter so long as we are together now?

MRS. G. (Looking round the horizon.) Yes. Only you and I--I and you--in the whole wide, wide world until the end. (Sees the line of the Snows.) How big and quiet the hills look! D'you think they care for us?

CAPT. G. 'Can't say I've consulted em particularly. I care, and that's enough for me.

MRS. G. (Drawing nearer to him.) Yes, now--but afterward. What's that little black blur on the Snows?

CAPT. G. A snowstorm, forty miles away. You'll see it move, as the wind carries it across the face of that spur and then it will be all gone.

MRS. G. And then it will be all gone. (Shivers.)

CAPT. G. (Anxiously.) Not chilled, pet, are you? Better let me get your cloak.

MRS. G. No. Don't leave me, Phil. Stay here. I believe I am afraid. Oh, why are the hills so horrid! Phil, promise me that you'll always love me.

CAPT. G. What's the trouble, darling? I can't promise any more than I have; but I'll promise that again and again if you like.

MRs. G. (Her head on his shoulder.) Say it, then--say it! N-no--don't!

The--the--eagles would laugh. (Recovering.) My husband, you've married a little goose.

CAPT. G. (Very tenderly.) Have I? I am content whatever she is, so long as she is mine.

MRS. G. (Quickly.) Because she is yours or because she is me mineself?

CAPT. G. Because she is both. (Piteously.) I'm not clever, dear, and I don't think I can make myself understood properly.

MRS. G. I understand. Pip, will you tell me something?

CAPT. G. Anything you like. (Aside.) I wonder what's coming now.

MRS. G. (Haltingly, her eyes 'owered.) You told me once in the old days--centuries and centuries ago--that you had been engaged before. I didn't say anything--then.

CAPT. G. (Innocently.) Why not?

MRS. G. (Raising her eyes to his.) Because--because I was afraid of losing you, my heart. But now--tell about it--please.

CAPT. G. There's nothing to tell. I was awf'ly old then--nearly two and twenty--and she was quite that.

MRS. G. That means she was older than you. I shouldn't like her to have been younger. Well?

CAPT. G. Well, I fancied myself in love and raved about a bit, and--oh, yes, by Jove! I made up poetry. Ha! Ha!

MRS. G. You never wrote any for me! What happened?

CAPT. G. I came out here, and the whole thing went phut. She wrote to say that there had been a mistake, and then she married.

MRS. G. Did she care for you much?

CAPT. G. No. At least she didn't show it as far as I remember.

MRS. G. As far as you remember! Do you remember her name? (Hears it and bows her head.) Thank you, my husband.

CAPT. G. Who but you had the right? Now, Little Featherweight, have you ever been mixed up in any dark and dismal tragedy?

MRS. G. If you call me Mrs. Gadsby, p'raps I'll tell.

CAPT. G. (Throwing Parade rasp into his voice.) Mrs. Gadsby, confess!

MRS. G. Good Heavens, Phil! I never knew that you could speak in that terrible voice.

CAPT. G. You don't know half my accomplishments yet. Wait till we are settled in the Plains, and I'll show you how I bark at my troop. You were going to say, darling?

MRS. G. I--I don't like to, after that voice. (Tremulously.) Phil, never you dare to speak to me in that tone, whatever I may do!

CAPT. G. My poor little love! Why, you're shaking all over. I am so sorry. Of course I never meant to upset you Don't tell me anything, I'm a brute.

MRS. G. No, you aren't, and I will tell--There was a man.

CAPT. G. (Lightly.) Was there? Lucky man!

MRS. G. (In a whisper.) And I thought I cared for him.

CAPT. G. Still luckier man! Well?

MRS. G. And I thought I cared for him--and I didn't--and then you came--and I cared for you very, very much indeed. That's all. (Face hidden.) You aren't angry, are you?

CAPT. G. Angry? Not in the least. (Aside.) Good Lord, what have I done to deserve this angel?

MRS. G. (Aside.) And he never asked for the name! How funny men are! But perhaps it's as well.

CAPT. G. That man will go to heaven because you once thought you cared for him. 'Wonder if you'll ever drag me up there?

MRS. G. (Firmly.) 'Sha'n't go if you don't.

CAPT. G. Thanks. I say, Pussy, I don't know much about your religious beliefs. You were brought up to believe in a heaven and all that, weren't you?

MRS. G. Yes. But it was a pincushion heaven, with hymn-books in all the pews.

CAPT. G. (Wagging his head with intense conviction.) Never mind. There is a pukka heaven.

MRS. G. Where do you bring that message from, my prophet?

CAPT. G. Here! Because we care for each other. So it's all right.

Mrs. G. (As a troop of langurs crash through the branches.) So it's all right. But Darwin says that we came from those!

CAPT. G. (Placidly.) Ah! Darwin was never in love with an angel. That settles it. Sstt, you brutes! Monkeys, indeed! You shouldn't read those books.

MRS. G. (Folding her hands.) If it pleases my Lord the King to issue proclamation.

CAPT. G. Don't, dear one. There are no orders between us. Only I'd rather you didn't. They lead to nothing, and bother people's heads.

MRS. G. Like your first engagement.

CAPT. G. (With an immense calm.) That was a necessary evil and led to you. Are you nothing?

MRS. G. Not so very much, am I?

CAPT. G. All this world and the next to me.

MRS. G. (Very softly.) My boy of boys! Shall I tell you something?

CAPT. G. Yes, if it's not dreadful--about other men.

MRS. G. It's about my own bad little self.

CAPT. G. Then it must be good. Go on, dear.

MRS. G. (Slowly.) I don't know why I'm telling you, Pip; but if ever you marry again-(Interlude.) Take your hand from my mouth or I'll bite! In the future, then remember--I don't know quite how to put it!

CAPT. G. (Snorting indignantly.) Don't try. "Marry again," indeed!

MRS. G. I must. Listen, my husband. Never, never, never tell your wife anything that you do not wish her to remember and think over all her life. Because a woman--yes, I am a woman--can't forget.

CAPT. G. By Jove, how do you know that?

MRS. G. (Confusedly.) I don't. I'm only guessing. I am--I was--a silly little girl; but I feel that I know so much, oh, so very much more than you, dearest. To begin with, I'm your wife.

CAPT. G. So I have been led to believe.

MRS. G. And I shall want to know every one of your secrets--to share everything you know with you. (Stares round desperately.)

CAPT. G. So you shall, dear, so you shall--but don't look like that.

MRS. G. For your own sake don't stop me, Phil. I shall never talk to you in this way again. You must not tell me! At least, not now. Later on, when I'm an old matron it won't matter, but if you love me, be very good to me now; for this part of my life I shall never forget! Have I made you understand?

CAPT. G. I think so, child. Have I said anything yet that you disapprove of?

MRS. G. Will you be very angry? That--that voice, and what you said about the engagement--

CAPT. G. But you asked to be told that, darling.

MRS. G. And that's why you shouldn't have told me! You must be the
Judge, and, oh, Pip, dearly as I love you, I shan't be able to help you!
I shall hinder you, and you must judge in spite of me!

CAPT. G. (Meditatively.) We have a great many things to find out
together, God help us both--say so, Pussy--but we shall understand each
other better every day; and I think I'm beginning to see now. How in the
world did you come to know just the importance of giving me just that
lead?

MRS. G. I've told you that I don't know. Only somehow it seemed that, in
all this new life, I was being guided for your sake as well as my own.

CAPT. G. (Aside.) Then Mafilin was right! They know, and we--we're blind
all of us. (Lightly.) 'Getting a little beyond our depth, dear, aren't
we? I'll remember, and, if I fail, let me be punished as I deserve.

MRS. G. There shall be no punishment. We'll start into life together
from here--you and I--and no one else.

CAPT. G. And no one else. (A pause.) Your eyelashes are all wet, Sweet?
Was there ever such a quaint little Absurdity?

MRS. G. Was there ever such nonsense talked before?

CAPT. G. (Knocking the ashes out of his pipe.) 'Tisn't what we say, it's
what we don't say, that helps. And it's all the profoundest philosophy.
But no one would understand--even if it were put into a book.

MRS. G. The idea! No--only we ourselves, or people like ourselves--if there are any people like us.

CAPT. G. (Magisterially.) All people, not like ourselves, are blind idiots.

MRS. G. (Wiping her eyes.) Do you think, then, that there are any people as happy as we are?

CAPT. G. 'Must be--unless we've appropriated all the happiness in the world.

MRS. G. (Looking toward Simla.) Poor dears! Just fancy if we have!

CAPT. G. Then we'll hang on to the whole show, for it's a great deal too jolly to lose--eh, wife o' mine?

MRS. G. O Pip! Pip! How much of you is a solemn, married man and how much a horrid slangy schoolboy?

CAPT. G. When you tell me how much of you was eighteen last birthday and how much is as old as the Sphinx and twice as mysterious, perhaps I'll attend to you. Lend me that banjo. The spirit moveth me to jowl at the sunset.

MRS. G. Mind! It's not tuned. Ah! How that jars!

CAPT G. (Turning pegs.) It's amazingly different to keep a banjo to proper pitch.

MRS. G. It's the same with all musical instruments, What shall it be?

CAPT. G. "Vanity," and let the hills hear. (Sings through the first and hal' of the second verse. Turning to MRS. G.) Now, chorus! Sing, Pussy!

BOTH TOGETHER. (Con brio, to the horror of the monkeys who are settling for the night.)--

"Vanity, all is Vanity," said Wisdom, scorning me--
I clasped my true Love's tender hand and answered frank and free-ee
"If this be Vanity who'd be wise? If this be Vanity who'd be wise?
If this be Vanity who'd be wi-ise (Crescendo.) Vanity let it be!"

MRS. G. (Defiantly to the grey of the evening sky.) "Vanity let it be!"

ECHO. (Prom the Fagoo spur.) Let it be!

FATIMA

And you may go in every room of the house and see everything that is there, but into the Blue Room you must not go.--The Story of Blue Beard.

SCENE.--The GADSBYS' bungalow in the Plains. Time, 11 A. M. on a Sunday morning. Captain GADSBY, in his shirt-sleeves, is bending over a complete set of Hussar's equipment, from saddle to picketing-rope, which is neatly spread over the floor of his study. He is smoking an unclean briar, and his forehead is puckered with thought.

CAPT. G. (To himself, fingering a headstall.) Jack's an ass. There's enough brass on this to load a mule--and, if the Americans know anything about anything, it can be cut down to a bit only. 'Don't want the watering-bridle, either. Humbug!-Half a dozen sets of chains and pulleys for one horse! Rot! (Scratching his head.) Now, let's consider it all over from the be-ginning. By Jove, I've forgotten the scale of weights! Ne'er mind. 'Keep the bit only, and eliminate every boss from the crupper to breastplate. No breastplate at all. Simple leather strap across the breast-like the Russians. Hi! Jack never thought of that!

MRS. G. (Entering hastily, her hand bound in a cloth.) Oh, Pip, I've scalded my hand over that horrid, horrid Tiparee jam!

CAPT. G. (Absently.) Eh! Wha-at?

MRS. G. (With round-eyed reproach.) I've scalded it aw-fully! Aren't you sorry? And I did so want that jam to jam properly.

CAPT. G. Poor little woman! Let me kiss the place and make it well. (Unrolling bandage.) You small sinner! Where's that scald? I can't see it.

MRS. G. On the top of the little finger. There!--It's a most 'normous big burn!

CAPT. G. (Kissing little finger.) Baby! Let Hyder look after the jam. You know I don't care for sweets.

MRS. G. In-deed?--Pip!

CAPT. G. Not of that kind, anyhow. And now run along, Minnie, and leave me to my own base devices. I'm busy.

MRS. G. (Calmly settling herself in long chair.) So I see. What a mess you're making! Why have you brought all that smelly leather stuff into the house?

CAPT. G. To play with. Do you mind, dear?

MRS. G. Let me play too. I'd like it.

CAPT. G. I'm afraid you wouldn't. Pussy--Don't you think that jam will burn, or whatever it is that jam does when it's not looked after by a clever little housekeeper?

MRS. G. I thought you said Hyder could attend to it. I left him in the veranda, stirring--when I hurt myself so.

CAPT. G. (His eye returning to the equipment.) Po-oor little woman!--Three pounds four and seven is three eleven, and that can be cut down to two eight, with just a lee-tle care, without weakening anything. Farriery is all rot in incompetent hands. What's the use of a shoe-case when a man's scouting? He can't stick it on with a lick-like a stamp--the shoe! Skittles--

MRS. G. What's skittles? Pah! What is this leather cleaned with?

CAPT. G. Cream and champagne and--Look here, dear, do you really want to talk to me about anything important?

MRS. G. No. I've done my accounts, and I thought I'd like to see what you're doing.

CAPT. G. Well, love, now you've seen and--Would you mind?--That is to say--Minnie, I really am busy.

MRS. G. You want me to go?

CAPT. G, Yes, dear, for a little while. This tobacco will hang in your dress, and saddlery doesn't interest you.

MRS. G. Everything you do interests me, Pip.

CAPT. G. Yes, I know, I know, dear. I'll tell you all about it some day when I've put a head on this thing. In the meantime--

MRS. G. I'm to be turned out of the room like a troublesome child?

CAPT. G. No-o. I don't mean that exactly. But, you see, I shall be tramping up and down, shifting these things to and fro, and I shall be in your way. Don't you think so?

MRS. G. Can't I lift them about? Let me try. (Reaches forward to trooper's saddle.)

CAPT. G. Good gracious, child, don't touch it. You'll hurt yourself. (Picking up saddle.) Little girls aren't expected to handle numdahs. Now, where would you like it put? (Holds saddle above his head.)

MRS. G. (A break in her voice.) Nowhere. Pip, how good you are--and how strong! Oh, what's that ugly red streak inside your arm?

CAPT. G. (Lowering saddle quickly.) Nothing. It's a mark of sorts. (Aside.) And Jack's coming to tiffin with his notions all cut and dried!

MRS. G. I know it's a mark, but I've never seen it before. It runs all up the arm. What is it?

CAPT. G. A cut--if you want to know.

MRS. G. Want to know! Of course I do! I can't have my husband cut to pieces in this way. How did it come? Was it an accident? Tell me, Pip.

CAPT. G. (Grimly.) No. 'Twasn't an accident. I got it--from a man--in Afghanistan.

MRS. G. In action? Oh, Pip, and you never told me!

CAPT. G. I'd forgotten all about it.

MRS. G. Hold up your arm! What a horrid, ugly scar! Are you sure it doesn't hurt now! How did the man give it you?

CAPT. G. (Desperately looking at his watch.) With a knife. I came down--old Van Loo did, that's to say--and fell on my leg, so I couldn't run. And then this man came up and began chopping at me as I sprawled.

MRS. G. Oh, don't, don't! That's enough!--Well, what happened?

CAPT. G. I couldn't get to my holster, and Mafflin came round the corner and stopped the performance.

MRS. G. How? He's such a lazy man, I don't believe he did.

CAPT. G. Don't you? I don't think the man had much doubt about it. Jack cut his head off.

MRS. G. Cut-his-head-off! "With one blow," as they say in the books?

CAPT. G. I'm not sure. I was too interested in myself to know much about it. Anyhow, the head was off, and Jack was punching old Van Loo in the ribs to make him get up. Now you know all about it, dear, and now--

MRS. G. You want me to go, of course. You never told me about this, though I've been married to you for ever so long; and you never would have told me if I hadn't found out; and you never do tell me anything about yourself, or what you do, or what you take an interest in.

CAPT. G. Darling, I'm always with you, aren't I?

MRS. G. Always in my pocket, you were going to say. I know you are; but you are always thinking away from me.

CAPT. G. (Trying to hide a smile.) Am I? I wasn't aware of it. I'm awf'ly sorry.

MRS. G. (Piteously.) Oh, don't make fun of me! Pip, you know what I mean. When you are reading one of those things about Cavalry, by that idiotic Prince--why doesn't he be a Prince instead of a stable-boy?

CAPT. G. Prince Kraft a stable-boy--Oh, my Aunt! Never mind, dear. You were going to say?

MRS. G. It doesn't matter; you don't care for what I say. Only--only you get up and walk about the room, staring in front of you, and then Mafflin comes in to dinner, and after I'm in the drawing-room I can hear you and him talking, and talking, and talking, about things I can't understand, and--oh, I get so tired and feel so lonely!--I don't want to complain and be a trouble, Pip; but I do indeed I do!

CAPT. G. My poor darling! I never thought of that. Why don't you ask some nice people in to dinner?

MRS. G. Nice people! Where am I to find them? Horrid frumps! And if I did, I shouldn't be amused. You know I only want you.

CAPT, G. And you have me surely, Sweetheart?

MRS. G. I have not! Pip why don't you take me into your life?

CAPT. G. More than I do? That would be difficult, dear.

MRS. G. Yes, I suppose it would--to you. I'm no help to you--no companion to you; and you like to have it so.

CAPT. G. Aren't you a little unreasonable, Pussy?

MRS. G. (Stamping her foot.) I'm the most reasonable woman in the world--when I'm treated properly.

CAPT. G. And since when have I been treating you improperly?

MRS. G. Always--and since the beginning. You know you have.

CAPT. G. I don't; but I'm willing to be convinced.

MRS. G. (Pointing to saddlery.) There!

CAPT. G. How do you mean?

MRS. G. What does all that mean? Why am I not to be told? Is it so precious?

CAPT. G. I forget its exact Government value just at present. It means that it is a great deal too heavy.

MRS. G. Then why do you touch it?

CAPT. G. To make it lighter. See here, little love, I've one notion and Jack has another, but we are both agreed that all this equipment is about thirty pounds too heavy. The thing is how to cut it down without weakening any part of it, and, at the same time, allowing the trooper to carry everything he wants for his own comfort-socks and shirts and things of that kind.

MRS. G. Why doesn't he pack them in a little trunk?

CAPT. G. (Kissing her.) Oh, you darling! Pack them in a little trunk, indeed! Hussars don't carry trunks, and it's a most important thing to make the horse do all the carrying.

MRS. G. But why need you bother about it? You're not a trooper.

CAPT. G. No; but I command a few score of him; and equipment is nearly everything in these days.

MRS. G. More than me?

CAPT. G. Stupid! Of course not; but it's a matter that I'm tremendously interested in, because if I or Jack, or I and Jack, work out some sort of lighter saddlery and all that, it's possible that we may get it adopted.

MRS. G. How?

CAPT. G. Sanctioned at Home, where they will make a sealed pattern--a pattern that all the saddlers must copy--and so it will be used by all the regiments.

MRS. G. And that interests you?

CAPT. G. It's part of my profession, y'know, and my profession is a good deal to me. Everything in a soldier's equipment is important, and if we can improve that equipment, so much the better for the soldiers and for us.

MRS. G. Who's "us"?

CAPT. G. Jack and I; only Jack's notions are too radical. What's that big sigh for, Minnie?

MRS. G. Oh, nothing--and you've kept all this a secret from me! Why?

CAPT. G. Not a secret, exactly, dear. I didn't say anything about it to you because I didn't think it would amuse you.

MRS. G. And am I only made to be amused?

CAPT. G. No, of course. I merely mean that it couldn't interest you.

MRS. G. It's your work and--and if you'd let me, I'd count all these things up. If they are too heavy, you know by how much they are too heavy, and you must have a list of things made out to your scale of lightness, and--

CAPT. G. I have got both scales somewhere in my head; but it's hard to tell how light you can make a head-stall, for instance, until you've actually had a model made.

MRS. G. But if you read out the list, I could copy it down, and pin it up there just above your table. Wouldn't that do?

CAPT. G. It would be awf'ly nice, dear, but it would be giving you trouble for nothing. I can't work that way. I go by rule of thumb. I know the present scale of weights, and the other one--the one that I'm trying to work to--will shift and vary so much that I couldn't be certain, even if I wrote it down.

MRS. G. I'm so sorry. I thought I might help. Is there anything else that I could be of use in?

CAPT. G. (Looking round the room.) I can't think of anything. You're always helping me you know.

MRS. G. Am I? How?

CAPT. G. You are of course, and as long as you're near me--I can't explain exactly, but it's in the air.

MRS. G. And that's why you wanted to send me away?

CAPT. G. That's only when I'm trying to do work--grubby work like this.

MRS. G. Mafflin's better, then, isn't he?

CAPT. G. (Rashly.) Of course he is. Jack and I have been thinking along the same groove for two or three years about this equipment. It's our hobby, and it may really be useful some day.

MRS. G. (After a pause.) And that's all that you have away from me?

CAPT. G. It isn't very far away from you now. Take care the oil on that bit doesn't come off on your dress.

MRS. G. I wish--I wish so much that I could really help you. I believe I could--if I left the room. But that's not what I mean.

CAPT. G. (Aside.) Give me patience! I wish she would go. (Aloud.) I as-sure you you can't do anything for me, Minnie, and I must really settle down to this. Where's my pouch?

MRS. G. (Crossing to writing-table.) Here you are, Bear. What a mess you keep your table in!

CAPT. G. Don't touch it. There's a method in my madness, though you mightn't think of it.

MRS. G. (At table.) I want to look--Do you keep accounts, Pip?

CAPT. G. (Bending over saddlery.) Of a sort. Are you rummaging among the Troop papers? Be careful.

MRs. G. Why? I sha'n't disturb anything. Good gracious! I had no idea that you had anything to do with so many sick horses.

CAPT. G. 'Wish I hadn't, but they insist on falling sick. Minnie, if

I were you I really should not investigate those papers. You may come across something that you won't like.

MRS. G. Why will you always treat me like a child? I know I'm not displacing the horrid things.

CAPT. G. (Resignedly.) Very well, then. Don't blame me if anything happens. Play with the table and let me go on with the saddlery. (Slipping hand into trousers-pocket.) Oh, the deuce!

MRS. G. (Her back to G.) What's that for?

CAPT. G. Nothing. (Aside.) There's not much in it, but I wish I'd torn it up.

MRS. G. (Turning over contents of table.) I know you'll hate me for this; but I do want to see what your work is like. (A pause.) Pip, what are "farcybuds"?

CAPT. G. Hab! Would you really like to know? They aren't pretty things.

MRS. G. This Journal of Veterinary Science says they are of "absorbing interest." Tell me.

CAPT. G. (Aside.) It may turn her attention.

Gives a long and designedly loathsome account of glanders and farcy.

MRS. G. Oh, that's enough. Don't go on!

CAPT. G. But you wanted to know--Then these things suppurate and matterate and spread--

MRS. G. Pin, you're making me sick! You're a horrid, disgusting schoolboy.

CAPT. G. (On his knees among the bridles.) You asked to be told. It's not my fault if you worry me into talking about horrors.

MRS. G. Why didn't you say--No?

CAPT. G. Good Heavens, child! Have you come in here simply to bully me?

MRS. G. I bully you? How could I! You're so strong. (Hysterically.) Strong enough to pick me up and put me outside the door and leave me there to cry. Aren't you?

CAPT. G. It seems to me that you're an irrational little baby. Are you quite well?

MRS. G. Do I look ill? (Returning to table). Who is your lady friend with the big grey envelope and the fat monogram outside?

CAPT. G. (Aside.) Then it wasn't locked up, confound it. (Aloud.) "God made her, therefore let her pass for a woman." You remember what farcybuds are like?

MRS. G. (Showing envelope.) This has nothing to do with them. I'm going to open it. May I?

CAPT. G. Certainly, if you want to. I'd sooner you didn't though. I don't ask to look at your letters to the Deer-court girl.

MRS. G. You'd better not, Sir! (Takes letter from envelope.) Now, may I look? If you say no, I shall cry.

CAPT. G. You've never cried in my knowledge of you, and I don't believe you could.

MRS. G. I feel very like it to-day, Pip. Don't be hard on me. (Reads letter.) It begins in the middle, without any "Dear Captain Gadsby," or anything. How funny!

CAPT. G. (Aside.) No, it's not Dear Captain Gadsby, or anything, now. How funny!

MRS. G. What a strange letter! (Reads.) "And so the moth has come too near the candle at last, and has been singed into--shall I say Respectability? I congratulate him, and hope he will be as happy as he deserves to be." What does that mean? Is she congratulating you about our marriage?

CAPT. G. Yes, I suppose so.

MRS. G. (Still reading letter.) She seems to be a particular friend of yours.

CAPT. G. Yes. She was an excellent matron of sorts--a Mrs. Herriott--wife of a Colonel Herriott. I used to know some of her people at Home long ago--before I came out.

MRS. G. Some Colonel's wives are young--as young as me. I knew one who was younger.

CAPT. G. Then it couldn't have been Mrs. Herriott. She was old enough to have been your mother, dear.

MRS. G. I remember now. Mrs. Scargill was talking about her at the Dutfins' tennis, before you came for me, on Tuesday. Captain Mafflin said she was a "dear old woman." Do you know, I think Mafilin is a very clumsy man with his feet.

CAPT. G. (Aside.) Good old Jack! (Aloud.) Why, dear?

MRS. G. He had put his cup down on the ground then, and he literally stepped into it. Some of the tea spirted over my dress--the grey one. I meant to tell you about it before.

CAPT. G. (Aside.) There are the makings of a strategist about Jack though his methods are coarse. (Aloud.) You'd better get a new dress, then. (Aside.) Let us pray that that will turn her.

MRS. G. Oh, it isn't stained in the least. I only thought that I'd tell you. (Returning to letter.) What an extraordinary person! (Reads.) "But need I remind you that you have taken upon yourself a charge of wardship"--what in the world is a charge of wardship?--"which as you yourself know, may end in Consequences"--

CAPT. G. (Aside.) It's safest to let em see everything as they come across it; but 'seems to me that there are exceptions to the rule. (Aloud.) I told you that there was nothing to be gained from rearranging my table.

MRS. G. (Absently.) What does the woman mean? She goes on talking about Consequences--"almost inevitable Consequences" with a capital C-- for half a page. (Flushing scarlet.) Oh, good gracious! How abominable!

CAPT. G. (Promptly.) Do you think so? Doesn't it show a sort of motherly interest in us? (Aside.) Thank Heaven. Harry always wrapped her meaning up safely! (Aloud.) Is it absolutely necessary to go on with the letter, darling?

MRS. G. It's impertinent--it's simply horrid. What right has this woman to write in this way to you? She oughtn't to.

CAPT. G. When you write to the Deercourt girl, I notice that you generally fill three or four sheets. Can't you let an old woman babble on paper once in a way? She means well.

MRS. G. I don't care. She shouldn't write, and if she did, you ought to have shown me her letter.

CAPT. G. Can't you understand why I kept it to myself, or must I explain at length--as I explained the farcybuds?

MRS. G. (Furiously.) Pip I hate you! This is as bad as those idiotic saddle-bags on the floor. Never mind whether it would please me or not, you ought to have given it to me to read.

CAPT. G. It comes to the same thing. You took it yourself.

MRS. G. Yes, but if I hadn't taken it, you wouldn't have said a word. I think this Harriet Herriott--it's like a name in a book--is an interfering old Thing.

CAPT. G. (Aside.) So long as you thoroughly understand that she is old, I don't much care what you think. (Aloud.) Very good, dear. Would you like to write and tell her so? She's seven thousand miles away.

MRS. G. I don't want to have anything to do with her, but you ought to have told me. (Turning to last page of letter.) And she patronizes me, too. I've never seen her! (Reads.) "I do not know how the world stands with you; in all human probability I shall never know; but whatever I may have said before, I pray for her sake more than for yours that all may be well. I have learned what misery means, and I dare not wish that any one dear to you should share my knowledge."

CAPT. G. Good God! Can't you leave that letter alone, or, at least, can't you refrain from reading it aloud? I've been through it once. Put it back on 'he desk. Do you hear me?

MRS. G. (Irresolutely.) I sh-sha'n't! (Looks at G.'s eyes.) Oh, Pip, please! I didn't mean to make you angry--'Deed, I didn't. Pip, I'm so sorry. I know I've wasted your time--CAPT. G. (Grimly.) You have. Now, will you be good enough to go--if there is nothing more in my room that you are anxious to pry into?

MRS. G. (Putting out her hands.) Oh, Pip, don't look at me like that! I've never seen you look like that before and it hu-urts me! I'm sorry. I oughtn't to have been here at all, and--and--and--(sobbing.) Oh, be good to me! Be good to me! There's only you--anywhere! Breaks down in long chair, hiding face in cushions.

CAPT. G. (Aside.) She doesn't know how she flicked me on the raw. (Aloud, bending over chair.) I didn't mean to be harsh, dear--I didn't really. You can stay here as long as you please, and do what you please. Don't cry like that. You'll make yourself sick. (Aside.) What on earth has come over her? (Aloud.) Darling, what's the matter with you?

Mrs. G. (Her face still hidden.) Let me go--let me go to my own room. Only--only say you aren't angry with me.

CAPT. G. Angry with you, love! Of course not. I was angry with myself. I'd lost my temper over the saddlery--Don't hide your face, Pussy. I want to kiss it.

Bends lower, MRS. G. slides right arm round his neck. Several interludes and much sobbing.

MRS. G. (In a whisper.) I didn't mean about the jam when I came in to tell you--

CAPT'. G. Bother the jam and the equipment! (Interlude.)

MRS. G. (Still more faintly.) My finger wasn't scalded at all. I--wanted to speak to you about--about--something else, and--I didn't know how.

CAPT. G. Speak away, then. (Looking into her eyes.) Eh! Wha-at? Minnie! Here, don't go away! You don't mean?

MRS. G. (Hysterically, backing to portiere and hiding her face in its fold's.) The--the Almost Inevitable Consequences! (Flits through portiere as G. attempts to catch her, and bolts her self in her own room.)

CAPT. G. (His arms full of portiere.) Oh! (Sitting down heavily in chair.) I'm a brute--a pig--a bully, and a blackguard. My poor, poor little darling! "Made to be amused only?"--

THE VALLEY OF THE SHADOW
Knowing Good and Evil.

SCENE.--The GADSBYS' bungalow in the Plains, in June. Punkah--coolies asleep in veranda where Captain GADSBY is walking up and down. DOCTOR'S
trap in porch. JUNIOR CHAPLAIN drifting generally and uneasily through the house. Time, 3:40 A. M. Heat 94 degrees in veranda.

DOCTOR. (Coming into veranda and touching G. on the shoulder.) You had better go in and see her now.

CAPT. G. (The color of good cigar-ash.) Eb, wha-at? Oh, yes, of course. What did you say?

DOCTOR. (Syllable by syllable.) Go--in--to--the--room--and--see--her. She wants to speak to you. (Aside, testily.) I shall have him on my hands next.

JUNIOR CHAPLAIN. (In half-lighted dining room.) Isn't there any?--

DOCTOR. (Savagely.) Hsh, you little fool!

JUNIOR CHAPLAIN. Let me do my work. Gadsby, stop a minute! (Edges after G.)

DOCTOR. Wait till she sends for you at least--at least. Man alive, he'll kill you if you go in there! What are you bothering him for?

JUNIOR CHAPLAIN. (Coming into veranda.) I've given him a stiff brandy-peg. He wants it. You've forgotten him for the last ten hours and--forgotten yourself too.

CAPT. G. enters bedroom, which is lit by one night-lamp. Ayak on the floor pretending to be asleep.

VOICE. (From the bed.) All down the street--such bonfires! Ayah, go and put them out! (Appealingly.) How can I sleep with an installation of the C.I.E. in my room? No--not C.I.E. Something else. What was it?

CAPT. G. (Trying to control his voice.) Minnie, I'm here. (Bending over bed.) Don't you know me, Minnie? It's me--it's Phil--it's your husband.
VOICE. (Mechanically.) It's me--it's Phil--it's your husband.

CAPT. G. She doesn't know mel--It's your own husband, darling.

VOICE. Your own husband, darling. AYAH. (With an inspiration.) Memsahib understanding all I saying.

CAPT. G. Make her understand me then--quick!

AYAH. (Hand on MRS. G.'s forehead.) Memsahib! Captain Sahib here.

VOICE. Salaem do. (Fretfully.) I know I'm not fit to be seen.

AYAH. (Aside to G.) Say "marneen" same as breakfash.

CAPT. G. Good-morning, little woman. How are we to-day?

VOICE. That's Phil. Poor old Phil. (Viciously.) Phil, you fool, I can't see you. Come nearer.

CAPT. G. Minnie! Minnie! It's me--you know me?

VOICE. (Mockingly.) Of course I do. Who does not know the man who was so
cruel to his wife--almost the only one he ever had?

CAPT. G. Yes, dear. Yes--of course, of course. But won't you speak to him? He wants to speak to you so much.

VOICE. They'd never let him in. The Doctor would give darwaza bund even if he were in the house. He'll never come. (Despairingly.) O Judas! Judas! Judas!

CAPT. G. (Putting out his arms.) They have let him in, and he always was in the house Oh, my love--don't you know me?

VOICE. (In a half chant.) "And it came to pass at the eleventh hour that this poor soul repented." It knocked at the gates, but they were shut--tight as a plaster--a great, burning plaster They had pasted our marriage certificate all across the door, and it was made of red-hot iron--people really ought to be more careful, you know.

CAPT. G. What am I to do? (Taking her in his arms.) Minnie! speak to me--to Phil.

VOICE. What shall I say? Oh, tell me what to say before it's too late! They are all going away and I can't say anything.

CAPT. G. Say you know me! Only say you know me!

DOCTOR. (Who has entered quietly.) For pity's sake don't take it too much to heart, Gadsby. It's this way sometimes. They won't recognize. They say all sorts of queer things--don't you see?

CAPT. G. All right! All right! Go away now; she'll recognize me; you're bothering her. She must--mustn't she?

DOCTOR. She will before--Have I your leave to try?--

CAPT. G. Anything you please, so long as she'll know me. It's only a question of--hours, isn't it?

DOCTOR. (Professionally.) While there's life there's hope y'know. But don't build on it.

CAPT. G. I don't. Pull her together if it's possible. (Aside.) What have I done to deserve this?

DOCTOR. (Bending over bed.) Now, Mrs. Gadsby! We shall be all right tomorrow. You must take it, or I sha'n't let Phil see you. It isn't nasty, is it?

Voice. Medicines! Always more medicines! Can't you leave me alone?

CAPT. G. Oh, leave her in peace, Doc!

DOCTOR. (Stepping back,--aside.) May I be forgiven if I've none wrong. (Aloud.) In a few minutes she ought to be sensible; but I daren't tell you to look for anything. It's only--

CAPT. G. What? Go on, man.

DOCTOR. (In a whisper.) Forcing the last rally.

CAPT. G. Then leave us alone.

DOCTOR. Don't mind what she says at first, if you can. They--they-they turn against those they love most sometimes in this.--It's hard, but--

CAPT. G. Am I her husband or are you? Leave us alone for what time we have together.

VOICE. (Confidentially.) And we were engaged quite suddenly, Emma. I assure you that I never thought of it for a moment; but, oh, my little Me!--I don't know what I should have done if he hadn't proposed.

CAPT. G. She thinks of that Deercourt girl before she thinks of me. (Aloud.) Minnie!

VOICE. Not from the shops, Mummy dear. You can get the real leaves from Kaintu, and (laughing weakly) never mind about the blossoms--Dead white silk is only fit for widows, and I won't wear it. It's as bad as a winding sheet. (A long pause.)

CAPT. G. I never asked a favor yet. If there is anybody to listen to me, let her know me--even if I die too!

VOICE. (Very faintly.) Pip, Pip dear.

CAPT. G. I'm here, darling.

VOICE. What has happened? They've been bothering me so with medicines and things, and they wouldn't let you come and see me. I was never ill before. Am I ill now?

CAPT. G. You--you aren't quite well.

VOICE. How funny! Have I been ill long?

CAPT. G. Some day; but you'll be all right in a little time.

VOICE. Do you think so, Pip? I don't feel well and--Oh! what have they done to my hair?

CAPT. G. I d-d-on't know.

VOICE. They've cut it off. What a shame!

CAPT. G. It must have been to make your head cooler.

VOICE. Just like a boy's wig. Don't I look horrid?

CAPT. G. Never looked prettier in your life, dear. (Aside.) How am I to ask her to say good-bye?

VOICE. I don't feel pretty. I feel very ill. My heart won't work. It's nearly dead inside me, and there's a funny feeling in my eyes. Everything seems the same distance--you and the almirah and the table inside my eyes or miles away. What does it mean, Pip?

CAPT. G. You're a little feverish, Sweetheart--very feverish. (Breaking down.) My love! my love! How can I let you go?

VOICE. I thought so. Why didn't you tell me that at first?

CAPT. G. What?

VOICE. That I am going to--die.

CAPT. G. But you aren't! You sha'n't.

AYAH to punkah-coolie. (Stepping into veranda after a glance at the bed.). Punkah chor do! (Stop pulling the punkah.)

VOICE. It's hard, Pip. So very, very hard after one year--just one year.

(Wailing.) And I'm only twenty. Most girls aren't even married at twenty. Can't they do anything to help me? I don't want to die.

CAPT. G. Hush, dear. You won't.

VOICE. What's the use of talking? Help me! You've never failed me yet. Oh, Phil, help me to keep alive. (Feverishly.) I don't believe you wish me to live. You weren't a bit sorry when that horrid Baby thing died. I wish I'd killed it!
CAPT. G. (Drawing his hand across his forehead.) It's more than a man's meant to bear--it's not right. (Aloud.) Minnie, love, I'd die for you if it would help.

VOICE. No more death. There's enough already. Pip, don't you die too.

CAPT. G. I wish I dared.

VOICE. It says: "Till Death do us part." Nothing after that--and so it would be no use. It stops at the dying. Why does it stop there? Only such a very short life, too. Pip, I'm sorry we married.

CAPT. G. No! Anything but that, Mm!

VOICE. Because you'll forget and I'll forget. Oh, Pip, don't forget! I always loved you, though I was cross sometimes. If I ever did anything that you didn't like, say you forgive me now.

CAPT. G. You never did, darling. On my soul and honor you never did. I haven't a thing to forgive you.

VOICE. I sulked for a whole week about those petunias. (With a laugh.) What a little wretch I was, and how grieved you were! Forgive me that, Pp.

CAPT. G. There's nothing to forgive. It was my fault. They were too near the drive. For God's sake don't talk so, Minnie! There's such a lot to say and so little time to say it in.

VOICE. Say that you'll always love me--until the end.

CAPT. G. Until the end. (Carried away.) It's a lie. It must be, because we've loved each other. This isn't the end.
VOICE. (Relapsing into semi-delirium.) My Church-service has an ivory-cross on the back, and it says so, so it must be true. "Till Death do us part."--but that's a lie. (With a parody of G.'s manner.) A damned lie! (Recklessly.) Yes, I can swear as well as a Trooper, Pip. I can't make my head think, though. That's because they cut off my hair. How can one think with one's head all fuzzy? (Pleadingly.) Hold me, Pip! Keep me with you always and always. (Relapsing.) But if you marry the Thorniss girl when I'm dead, I'll come back and howl under our bedroom window all night. Oh, bother! You'll think I'm a jackall. Pip, what time is it?

CAPT. G. A little before the dawn, dear.

VOICE. I wonder where I shall be this time to-morrow?

CAPT. G. Would you like to see the Padre?

VOICE. Why should I? He'd tell me that I am going to heaven; and that wouldn't be true, because you are here. Do you recollect when he upset the cream-ice all over his trousers at the Gassers' tennis?

CAPT. G. Yes, dear.

VOICE. I often wondered whether he got another pair of trousers; but then his are so shiny all over that you really couldn't tell unless you were told. Let's call him in and ask.

CAPT. G. (Gravely.) No. I don't think he'd like that. 'Your head comfy, Sweetheart?'

VOICE. (Faintly with a sigh of contentment.) Yeth! Gracious, Pip, when did you shave last? Your chin's worse than the barrel of a musical box.--No, don't lift it up. I like it. (A pause.) You said you've never cried at all. You're crying all over my cheek.
CAPT. G. I--I--I can't help it, dear.

VOICE. How funny! I couldn't cry now to save my life. (G. shivers.) I want to sing.

CAPT. G. Won't it tire you? 'Better not, perhaps.

VOICE. Why? I won't be bothered about. (Begins in a hoarse quaver)

"Minnie bakes oaten cake, Minnie brews ale, All because her Johnnie's coming home from the sea. (That's parade, Pip.) And she grows red as a rose, who was so pale; And 'Are you sure the church--clock goes?' says she."

(Pettishly.) I knew I couldn't take the last note. How do the bass chords run? (Puts out her hands and begins playing piano on the sheet.)

CAPT. G. (Catching up hands.) Ahh! Don't do that, Pussy, if you love me.

VOICE. Love you? Of course I do. Who else should it be? (A pause.)

VOICE. (Very clearly.) Pip, I'm going now. Something's choking me cruelly. (Indistinctly.) Into the dark--without you, my heart--But it's a lie, dear--we mustn't believe it.--Forever and ever, living or dead. Don't let me go, my husband--hold me tight.--They can't--whatever happens. (A cough.) Pip--my Pip! Not for always--and--so--soon! (Voice ceases.)

Pause of ten minutes. G. buries his face in the side of the bed while AYAH bends over bed from opposite side and feels MRS. G.'s breast and forehead.

CAPT. G. (Rising.) Doctor Sahib ko salaam do.
AYAH. (Still by bedside, with a shriek.) Ai! Ai! Tuta-phuta! My Memsahib! Not getting--not have got!--Pusseena agyal (The sweat has come.) (Fiercely to G.) TUM jao Doctor Sahib ko jaldi! (You go to the doctor.) Oh, my Memsahib!

DOCTOR. (Entering hastily.) Come away, Gadsby. (Bends over bed.) Eh! The Dev--What inspired you to stop the punkah? Get out, man--go away--wait outside! Go! Here, Ayah! (Over his shoulder to G.) Mind I promise nothing.

The dawn breaks as G. stumbles into the garden.

CAPT. M. (Rehung up at the gate on his way to parade and very soberly.) Old man, how goes?

CAPT. G. (Dazed.) I don't quite know. Stay a bit. Have a drink or something. Don't run away. You're just getting amusing. Ha! ha!

CAPT. M. (Aside.) What am I let in for? Gaddy has aged ten years in the night.

CAPT. G. (Slowly, fingering charger's headstall.) Your curb's too loose.

CAPT. M. So it is. Put it straight, will you? (Aside.) I shall be late for parade. Poor Gaddy.

CAPT. G. links and unlinks curb-chain aimlessly, and finally stands staring toward the veranda. The day brightens.

DOCTOR. (Knocked out of professional gravity, tramping across flower-beds and shaking G's hands.) It'--it's--it's!--Gadsby, there's a fair chance--a dashed fair chance. The flicker, y'know. The sweat, y'know I saw how it would be. The punkab, y'know. Deuced clever woman that Ayah of yours. Stopped the punkab just at the right time. A dashed good chance! No--you don't go in. We'll pull her through yet I promise on my reputation--under Providence. Send a man with this note to Bingle. Two heads better than one. 'Specially the Ayah! We'll pull her round. (Retreats hastily to house.)

CAPT. G. (His head on neck of M.'s charger.) Jack! I bub--bu--believe, I'm going to make a bu-bub-bloody exhibit of byself.

CAPT. M. (Sniffing openly and feeling in his left cuff.) I b-b-believe, I'b doing it already. Old bad, what cad I say? I'b as pleased as--Cod dab you, Gaddy! You're one big idiot and I'b adother. (Pulling himself together.) Sit tight! Here comes the Devil-dodger.

JUNIOR CHAPLAIN. (Who is not in the Doctor's confidence.) We--we are only men in these things, Gadsby. I know that I can say nothing now to help.

CAPT. M. (jealously.) Then don't say it Leave him alone. It's not bad enough to croak over. Here, Gaddy, take the chit to Bingle and ride hell-for-leather. It'll do you good. I can't go.

JUNIOR CHAPLAIN. Do him good! (Smiling.) Give me the chit and I'll drive. Let him lie down. Your horse is blocking my cart--please!

CAPT. M. (Slowly without reining back.) I beg your pardon--I'll apologize. On paper if you like.

JUNIOR CHAPLAIN. (Flicking M.'s charger.) That'll do, thanks. Turn in, Gadsby, and I'll bring Bingle back--ahem--"hell-for-leather."

CAPT. M. (Solus.) It would have served me right if he'd cut me across the face. He can drive too. I shouldn't care to go that pace in a bamboo cart. What a faith he must have in his Maker--of harness! Come hup, you brute! (Gallops off to parade, blowing his nose, as the sun rises.)

(INTERVAL OF' FIVE WEEKS.)

MRS. G. (Very white and pinched, in morning wrapper at break fast table.) How big and strange the room looks, and how glad I am to see it again! What dust, though! I must talk to the servants. Sugar, Pip? I've almost forgotten. (Seriously.) Wasn't I very ill?

CAPT. G. Iller than I liked. (Tenderly.) Oh, you bad little Pussy, what a start you gave me.

MRS. G. I'll never do it again.

CAPT. G. You'd better not. And now get those poor pale cheeks pink again, or I shall be angry. Don't try to lift the urn. You'll upset it. Wait. (Comes round to head of table and lifts urn.)

MRS. G. (Quickly.) Khitmatgar, howarchikhana see kettly lao. Butler, get a kettle from the cook-house. (Drawing down G.'s face to her own.) Pip dear, I remember.

CAPT. G. What?

MRS. G. That last terrible night.

CAPT'. G. Then just you forget all about it.

MRS. G. (Softly, her eyes filling.) Never. It has brought us very close together, my husband. There! (Interlude.) I'm going to give Junda a saree.

CAPT. G. I gave her fifty dibs.

MRS. G. So she told me. It was a 'normous reward. Was I worth it? (Several interludes.) Don't! Here's the khitmatgar.--Two lumps or one Sir?

THE SWELLING OF JORDAN

If thou hast run with the footmen and they have wearied thee, then how canst thou contend with horses? And if in the land of peace wherein thou trustedst they wearied thee, then how wilt thou do in the swelling of Jordan?

SCENE.--The GADSBYS' bungalow in the Plains, on a January morning. MRS.
G. arguing with bearer in back veranda.

CAPT. M. rides up.

CAPT. M. 'Mornin', Mrs. Gadsby. How's the Infant Phenomenon and the Proud Proprietor?

MRS. G. You'll find them in the front veranda; go through the house. I'm Martha just now.

CAPT. M, 'Cumbered about with cares of Khitmatgars? I fly.

Passes into front veranda, where GADSBY is watching GADSBY JUNIOR, aged
ten months, crawling about the matting.

CAPT. M. What's the trouble, Gaddy--spoiling an honest man's Europe morning this way? (Seeing G. JUNIOR.) By Jove, that yearling's comm' on amazingly! Any amount of bone below the knee there.

CAPT. G. Yes, he's a healthy little scoundrel. Don't you think his hair's growing?

CAPT. M. Let's have a look. Hi! Hst Come here, General Luck, and we'll report on you.

MRS. G. (Within.) What absurd name will you give him next? Why do you call him that?

CAPT. M. Isn't he our Inspector--General of Cavalry? Doesn't he come down in his seventeen-two perambulator every morning the Pink Hussars parade? Don't wriggle, Brigadier. Give us your private opinion on the way the third squadron went past. 'Trifle ragged, weren't they?

CAPT. G. A bigger set of tailors than the new draft I don't wish to see. They've given me more than my fair share--knocking the squadron out of shape. It's sickening!

CAPT. M. When you're in command, you'll do better, young 'un. Can't you walk yet? Grip my finger and try. (To G.) 'Twon't hurt his hocks, will it?

CAPT. G. Oh, no. Don't let him flop, though, or he'll lick all the blacking off your boots.

MRS. G. (Within.) Who's destroying my son's character?

CAPT. M. And my Godson's. I'm ashamed of you, Gaddy. Punch your father in the eye, Jack! Don't you stand it! Hit him again!

CAPT. G. (Sotto voce.) Put The Butcha down and come to the end of the veranda. I'd rather the Wife didn't hear--just now.

CAPT. M. You look awf'ly serious. Anything wrong?

CAPT. G. 'Depends on your view entirely. I say, Jack, you won't think more hardly of me than you can help, will you? Come further this way.--The fact of the matter is, that I've made up my mind--at least I'm thinking seriously of--cutting the Service.

CAPT. M. Hwhatt?

CAPT. G. Don't shout. I'm going to send in my papers.

CAPT. M. You! Are you mad?

CAPT. G. No--only married.

CAPT. M. Look here! What's the meaning of it all? You never intend to leave us. You can't. Isn't the best squadron of the best regiment of the best cavalry in all the world good enough for you?

CAPT. G. (Jerking his head over his shoulder.) She doesn't seem to thrive in this God-forsaken country, and there's The Butcha to be considered and all that, you know.

CAPT. M. Does she say that she doesn't like India?

CAPT. G. That's the worst of it. She won't for fear of leaving me.

CAPT. M. What are the Hills made for?

CAPT. G. Not for my wife, at any rate.

CAPT. M. You know too much, Gaddy, and--I don't like you any the better for it!

CAPT. G. Never mind that. She wants England, and The Butcha would be all the better for it. I'm going to chuck. You don't understand.

CAPT. M. (Hotly.) I understand this One hundred and thirty-seven new horse to be licked into shape somehow before Luck comes round again; a hairy-heeled draft who'll give more trouble than the horses; a camp next cold weather for a certainty; ourselves the first on the roster; the Russian shindy ready to come to a head at five minutes' notice, and you, the best of us all, backing out of it all! Think a little, Gaddy. You won't do it.

CAPT. G. Hang it, a man has some duties toward his family, I suppose.

CAPT. M. I remember a man, though, who told me, the night after Amdheran, when we were picketed under Jagai, and he'd left his sword--by the way, did you ever pay Ranken for that sword?--in an Utmanzai's head--that man told me that he'd stick by me and the Pinks as long as he lived. I don't blame him for not sticking by me--I'm not much of a man--but I do blame him for not sticking by the Pink Hussars.

CAPT. G. (Uneasily.) We were little more than boys then. Can't you see, Jack, how things stand? 'Tisn't as if we were serving for our bread. We've all of us, more or less, got the filthy lucre. I'm luckier than some, perhaps. There's no call for me to serve on.

CAPT. M. None in the world for you or for us, except the Regimental. If you don't choose to answer to that, of course--

CAPT. G. Don't be too hard on a man. You know that a lot of us only take up the thing for a few years and then go back to Town and catch on with the rest.

CAPT. M. Not lots, and they aren't some of Us.

CAPT. G. And then there are one's affairs at Home to be considered--my
place and the rents, and all that. I don't suppose my father can last
much longer, and that means the title, and so on.

CAPT. M. 'Fraid you won't be entered in the Stud Book correctly unless
you go Home? Take six months, then, and come out in October. If I could
slay off a brother or two, I s'pose I should be a Marquis of sorts.
Any fool can be that; but it needs men, Gaddy--men like you--to lead
flanking squadrons properly. Don't you delude yourself into the belief
that you're going Home to take your place and prance about among
pink-nosed Kabuli dowagers. You aren't built that way. I know better.

CAPT. G. A man has a right to live his life as happily as he can. You
aren't married.

CAPT. M. No--praise be to Providence and the one or two women who have
had the good sense to jawab me.

CAPT. G. Then you don't know what it is to go into your own room and see
your wife's head on the pillow, and when everything else is safe and the
house shut up for the night, to wonder whether the roof-beams won't give
and kill her.

CAPT. M. (Aside.) Revelations first and second! (Aloud.) So-o! I knew
a man who got squiffy at our Mess once and confided to me that he never
helped his wife on to her horse without praying that she'd break her neck
before she came back. All husbands aren't alike, you see.

CAPT. G. What on earth has that to do with my case? The man must ha' been mad, or his wife as bad as they make 'em.

CAPT. M. (Aside.) 'No fault of yours if either weren't all you say. You've forgotten the time when you were insane about the Herriott woman. You always were a good hand at forgetting. (Aloud.) Not more mad than men who go to the other extreme. Be reasonable, Gaddy. Your roof-beams are sound enough.

CAPT. G. That was only a way of speaking. I've been uneasy and worried about the Wife ever since that awful business three years ago--when--I nearly lost her. Can you wonder?

CAPT. M. Oh, a shell never falls twice in the same place. You've paid your toll to misfortune--why should your Wife be picked out more than anybody else's?

CAPT. G. I can talk just as reasonably as you can, but you don't understand--you don't understand. And then there's The Butcha. Deuce knows where the Ayah takes him to sit in the evening! He has a bit of a cough. Haven't you noticed it?

CAPT. M. Bosh! The Brigadier's jumping out of his skin with pure condition. He's got a muzzle like a rose-leaf and the chest of a two-year-old. What's demoralized you?

CAPT. G. Funk. That's the long and the short of it. Funk!

CAPT. M. But what is there to funk?

CAPT. G. Everything. It's ghastly.

CAPT. M. Ah! I see.

You don't want to fight, And by Jingo when we do, You've got the kid, you've got the Wife, You've got the money, too.

That's about the case, eh?

CAPT. G. I suppose that's it. But it's not br myself. It's because of them. At least I think it is.

CAPT. M. Are you sure? Looking at the matter in a cold-blooded light, the Wife is provided for even if you were wiped out tonight. She has an ancestral home to go to, money and the Brigadier to carry on the illustrious name.

CAPT. G. Then it is for myself or because they are part of me. You don't see it. My life's so good, so pleasant, as it is, that I want to make it quite safe. Can't you understand?

CAPT. M. Perfectly. "Shelter-pit for the Off'cer's charger," as they say in the Line.

CAPT. G. And I have everything to my hand to make it so. I'm sick of the strain and the worry for their sakes out here; and there isn't a single real difficulty to prevent my dropping it altogether. It'll only cost me--Jack, I hope you'll never know the shame that I've been going through for the past six months.

CAPT. M. Hold on there! I don't wish to be told. Every man has his moods and tenses sometimes.

CAPT. G. (Laughing bitterly.) Has he? What do you call craning over to see where your near-fore lands?

CAPT. M. In my case it means that I have been on the Considerable Bend, and have come to parade with a Head and a Hand. It passes in three strides.

CAPT. G. (Lowering voice.) It never passes with me, Jack. I'm always thinking about it. Phil Gadsby funking a fall on parade! Sweet picture, isn't it! Draw it for me.

CAPT. M. (Gravely.) Heaven forbid! A man like you can't be as bad as that. A fall is no nice thing, but one never gives it a thought.

CAPT. G. Doesn't one? Wait till you've got a wife and a youngster of your own, and then you'll know how the roar of the squadron behind you turns you cold all up the back.

CAPT. M. (Aside.) And this man led at Amdheran after Bagal Deasin went under, and we were all mixed up together, and he came out of the snow dripping like a butcher. (Aloud.) Skittles! The men can always open out, and you can always pick your way more or less. We haven't the dust to bother us, as the men have, and whoever heard of a horse stepping on a man?

CAPT. G. Never-as long as he can see. But did they open out for poor 'Errington?

CAPT. M. Oh, this is childish!

CAPT. G. I know it is, worse than that. I don't care. You've ridden Van Loo. Is he the sort of brute to pick his way-'specially when we're coming up in column of troop with any pace on?

CAPT. M. Once in a Blue Moon do we gallop in column of troop, and then only to save time. Aren't three lengths enough for you?

CAPT. G. Yes--quite enough. They just allow for the full development of the smash. I'm talking like a cur, I know: but I tell you that, for the past three months, I've felt every hoof of the squadron in the small of my back every time that I've led.

CAPT. M. But, Gaddy, this is awful!

CAPT. G. Isn't it lovely? Isn't it royal? A Captain of the Pink Hussars watering up his charger before parade like the blasted boozing Colonel of a Black Regiment!

CAPT. M. You never did!

CAPT. G. Once Only. He squelched like a mussuck, and the Troop--Sergeant-Major cocked his eye at me. You know old Haffy's eye. I was afraid to do it again.

CAPT. M. I should think so. That was the best way to rupture old Van Loo's tummy, and make him crumple you up. You knew that.

CAPT. G. I didn't care. It took the edge off him.

CAPT. M. "Took the edge off him"? Gaddy, you--you--you mustn't, you know! Think of the men.

CAPT. G. That's another thing I am afraid of. D'you s'pose they know?

CAPT. M. Let's hope not; but they're deadly quick to spot skirm--little things of that kind. See here, old man, send the Wife Home for the hot weather and come to Kashmir with me. We'll start a boat on the Dal or cross the Rhotang--shoot ibex or loaf--which you please. Only come! You're a bit off your oats and you're talking nonsense. Look at the Colonel--swag-bellied rascal that he is. He has a wife and no end of a bow-window of his own. Can any one of us ride round him--chalkstones and all? I can't, and I think I can shove a crock along a bit.

CAPT. G. Some men are different. I haven't any nerve. Lord help me, I haven't the nerve! I've taken up a hole and a half to get my knees well under the wallets. I can't help it. I'm so afraid of anything happening to me. On my soul, I ought to be broke in front of the squadron, for cowardice.

CAPT. M. Ugly word, that. I should never have the courage to own up.

CAPT. G. I meant to lie about my reasons when I began, but--I've got out of the habit of lying to you, old man. Jack, you won't?--But I know you won't.

CAPT. M. Of course not. (Half aloud.) The Pinks are paying dearly for their Pride.

CAPT. G. Eh! What-at?

CAPT. M. Don't you know? The men have called Mrs. Gadsby the Pride of the Pink Hussars ever since she came to us.

CAPT. G. 'Tisn't her fault. Don't think that. It's all mine.

CAPT. M. What does she say?

CAPT. G. I haven't exactly put it before her. She's the best little woman in the world, Jack, and all that--but she wouldn't counsel a man to stick to his calling if it came between him and her. At least, I think--

CAPT. M. Never mind. Don't tell her what you told me. Go on the Peerage and Landed-Gentry tack.

CAPT. G. She'd see through it. She's five times cleverer than I am.

CAPT. M. (Aside.) Then she'll accept the sacrifice and think a little bit worse of him for the rest of her days.

CAPT. G. (Absently.) I say, do you despise me?

CAPT. M. 'Queer way of putting it. Have you ever been asked that question? Think a minute. What answer used you to give?

CAPT. G. So bad as that? I'm not entitled to expect anything more, but it's a bit hard when one's best friend turns round and--

CAPT. M. So! have found But you will have consolations--Bailiffs and Drains and Liquid Manure and the Primrose League, and, perhaps, if you're lucky, the Colonelcy of a Yeomanry Cav-al-ry Regiment--all uniform and no riding, I believe. How old are you?

CAPT. G. Thirty-three. I know it's--

CAPT. M. At forty you'll be a fool of a J. P. landlord. At fifty you'll own a bath-chair, and The Brigadier, if he takes after you, will be fluttering the dovecotes of--what's the particular dunghill you're going to? Also, Mrs. Gadsby will be fat.

CAPT. G. (Limply.) This is rather more than a joke.

CAPT. M. D'you think so? Isn't cutting the Service a joke? It generally takes a man fifty years to arrive at it. You're quite right, though. It is more than a joke. You've managed it in thirty-three.

CAPT. G. Don't make me feel worse than I do. Will it satisfy you if I own that I am a shirker, a skrim-shanker, and a coward?

CAPT. M. It wil! not, because I'm the only man in the world who can talk to you like this without being knocked down. You mustn't take all that I've said to heart in this way. I only spoke--a lot of it at least--out of pure selfishness, because, because--Oh, damn it all, old man,--I don't know what I shall do without you. Of course, you've got the money and the place and all that--and there are two very good reasons why you should take care of yourself.

CAPT. G. 'Doesn't make it any sweeter. I'm backing out--I know I am. I always had a soft drop in me somewhere--and I daren't risk any danger to them.

CAPT. M. Why in the world should you? You're bound to think of your family-bound to think. Er--hmm. If I wasn't a younger son I'd go too--be shot if I wouldn't!

CAPT. G. Thank you, Jack. It's a kind lie, but it's the blackest you've told for some time. I know what I'm doing, and I'm going into it with my eyes open. Old man, I can't help it. What would you do if you were in my place?

CAPT. M. (Aside.) 'Couldn't conceive any woman getting permanently between me and the Regiment. (Aloud.) 'Can't say. 'Very likely I should do no better. I'm sorry for you--awf'ly sorry--but "if them's your sentiments," I believe, I really do, that you are acting wisely.

CAPT. G. Do you? I hope you do. (In a whisper.) Jack, be very sure of yourself before you marry. I'm an ungrateful ruffian to say this, but marriage--even as good a marriage as mine has been--hampers a man's work, it cripples his sword-arm, and oh, it plays Hell with his notions of duty. Sometimes--good and sweet as she is--sometimes I could wish that I had kept my freedom--No, I don't mean that exactly.

MRS. G. (Coming down veranda.) What are you wagging your head over, Pip?

CAPT. M. (Turning quickly.) Me, as usual. The old sermon. Your husband is recommending me to get married. 'Never saw such a one-ideaed man.

MRS. G. Well, why don't you? I dare say you would make some woman very happy.

CAPT. G. There's the Law and the Prophets, Jack. Never mind the Regiment. Make a woman happy. (Aside.) O Lord!

CAPT. M. We'll see. I must be off to make a Troop Cook desperately unhappy. I won't have the wily Hussar fed on Government Bullock Train shinbones--(Hastily.) Surely black ants can't be good for The Brigadier. He's picking em off the matting and eating 'em. Here, Senor Comandante Don Grubbynuse, come and talk to me. (Lifts G. JUNIOR in his arms.) 'Want my watch? You won't be able to put it into your mouth, but you can try. (G. JUNIOR drops watch, breaking dial and hands.)

MRS. G. Oh, Captain Mafflin, I am so sorry! Jack, you bad, bad little villain. Ahhh!

CAPT. M. It's not the least consequence, I assure you. He'd treat the world in the same way if he could get it into his hands. Everything's made to be played, with and broken, isn't it, young 'un?

* * * * *

MRS. G. Mafflin didn't at all like his watch being broken, though he was too polite to say so. It was entirely his fault for giving it to the child. Dem little puds are werry, werry feeble, aren't dey, by Jack-in-de-box? (To G.) What did he want to see you for?

CAPT. G. Regimental shop as usual.

MRS. G. The Regiment! Always the Regiment. On my word, I sometimes feel jealous of Mafflin.

CAPT. G. (Wearily.) Poor old Jack? I don't think you need. Isn't it time for The Butcha to have his nap? Bring a chair out here, dear. I've got some thing to talk over with you.

AND THIS IS THE END OF THE STORY OF THE GADSBYS

The Codes Of Hammurabi And Moses
W. W. Davies

QTY

The discovery of the Hammurabi Code is one of the greatest achievements of archaeology, and is of paramount interest, not only to the student of the Bible, but also to all those interested in ancient history...

Religion   **ISBN:** *1-59462-338-4*   **Pages:132**
MSRP $12.95

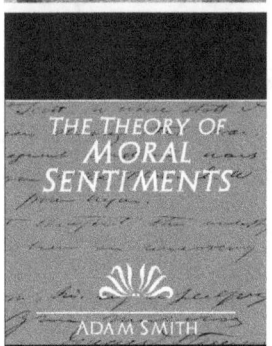

The Theory of Moral Sentiments
Adam Smith

QTY

This work from 1749. contains original theories of conscience amd moral judgment and it is the foundation for systemof morals.

Philosophy **ISBN:** *1-59462-777-0*   **Pages:536**
MSRP $19.95

Jessica's First Prayer
Hesba Stretton

QTY

In a screened and secluded corner of one of the many railway-bridges which span the streets of London there could be seen a few years ago, from five o'clock every morning until half past eight, a tidily set-out coffee-stall, consisting of a trestle and board, upon which stood two large tin cans, with a small fire of charcoal burning under each so as to keep the coffee boiling during the early hours of the morning when the work-people were thronging into the city on their way to their daily toil...

Childrens   **ISBN:** *1-59462-373-2*   **Pages:84**
MSRP $9.95

My Life and Work
Henry Ford

QTY

Henry Ford revolutionized the world with his implementation of mass production for the Model T automobile. Gain valuable business insight into his life and work with his own auto-biography... "We have only started on our development of our country we have not as yet, with all our talk of wonderful progress, done more than scratch the surface. The progress has been wonderful enough but..."

Biographies/   **ISBN:** *1-59462-198-5*   **Pages:300**
MSRP $21.95

The Art of Cross-Examination
Francis Wellman

QTY

I presume it is the experience of every author, after his first book is published upon an important subject, to be almost overwhelmed with a wealth of ideas and illustrations which could readily have been included in his book, and which to his own mind, at least, seem to make a second edition inevitable. Such certainly was the case with me; and when the first edition had reached its sixth impression in five months, I rejoiced to learn that it seemed to my publishers that the book had met with a sufficiently favorable reception to justify a second and considerably enlarged edition. ...

Pages:412

Reference   ISBN: *1-59462-647-2*   *MSRP $19.95*

On the Duty of Civil Disobedience
Henry David Thoreau

QTY

Thoreau wrote his famous essay, On the Duty of Civil Disobedience, as a protest against an unjust but popular war and the immoral but popular institution of slave-owning. He did more than write—he declined to pay his taxes, and was hauled off to gaol in consequence. Who can say how much this refusal of his hastened the end of the war and of slavery ?

Law   ISBN: *1-59462-747-9*   **Pages:48**
MSRP $7.45

Dream Psychology Psychoanalysis for Beginners
Sigmund Freud

QTY

Sigmund Freud, born Sigismund Schlomo Freud (May 6, 1856 - September 23, 1939), was a Jewish-Austrian neurologist and psychiatrist who co-founded the psychoanalytic school of psychology. Freud is best known for his theories of the unconscious mind, especially involving the mechanism of repression; his redefinition of sexual desire as mobile and directed towards a wide variety of objects; and his therapeutic techniques, especially his understanding of transference in the therapeutic relationship and the presumed value of dreams as sources of insight into unconscious desires.

Pages:196

Psychology   ISBN: *1-59462-905-6*   *MSRP $15.45*

The Miracle of Right Thought
Orison Swett Marden

QTY

Believe with all of your heart that you will do what you were made to do. When the mind has once formed the habit of holding cheerful, happy, prosperous pictures, it will not be easy to form the opposite habit. It does not matter how improbable or how far away this realization may see, or how dark the prospects may be, if we visualize them as best we can, as vividly as possible, hold tenaciously to them and vigorously struggle to attain them, they will gradually become actualized, realized in the life. But a desire, a longing without endeavor, a yearning abandoned or held indifferently will vanish without realization.

Pages:360

Self Help   ISBN: *1-59462-644-8*   *MSRP $25.45*

☐	**The Rosicrucian Cosmo-Conception Mystic Christianity** *by Max Heindel*	ISBN: *1-59462-188-8*	**$38.95**
	The Rosicrucian Cosmo-conception is not dogmatic, neither does it appeal to any other authority than the reason of the student. It is: not controversial, but is: sent forth in the, hope that it may help to clear...	New Age/Religion Pages 646	
☐	**Abandonment To Divine Providence** *by Jean-Pierre de Caussade*	ISBN: *1-59462-228-0*	**$25.95**
	"The Rev. Jean Pierre de Caussade was one of the most remarkable spiritual writers of the Society of Jesus in France in the 18th Century. His death took place at Toulouse in 1751. His works have gone through many editions and have been republished...	Inspirational/Religion Pages 400	
☐	**Mental Chemistry** *by Charles Haanel*	ISBN: *1-59462-192-6*	**$23.95**
	Mental Chemistry allows the change of material conditions by combining and appropriately utilizing the power of the mind. Much like applied chemistry creates something new and unique out of careful combinations of chemicals the mastery of mental chemistry...	New Age Pages 354	
☐	**The Letters of Robert Browning and Elizabeth Barret Barrett 1845-1846 vol II**	ISBN: *1-59462-193-4*	**$35.95**
	*by **Robert Browning** and **Elizabeth Barrett***	Biographies Pages 596	
☐	**Gleanings In Genesis (volume I)** *by Arthur W. Pink*	ISBN: *1-59462-130-6*	**$27.45**
	Appropriately has Genesis been termed "the seed plot of the Bible" for in it we have, in germ form, almost all of the great doctrines which are afterwards fully developed in the books of Scripture which follow...	Religion/Inspirational Pages 420	
☐	**The Master Key** *by L. W. de Laurence*	ISBN: *1-59462-001-6*	**$30.95**
	In no branch of human knowledge has there been a more lively increase of the spirit of research during the past few years than in the study of Psychology, Concentration and Mental Discipline. The requests for authentic lessons in Thought Control, Mental Discipline and...	New Age/Business Pages 422	
☐	**The Lesser Key Of Solomon Goetia** *by L. W. de Laurence*	ISBN: *1-59462-092-X*	**$9.95**
	This translation of the first book of the "Lernegton" which is now for the first time made accessible to students of Talismanic Magic was done, after careful collation and edition, from numerous Ancient Manuscripts in Hebrew, Latin, and French...	New Age/Occult Pages 92	
☐	**Rubaiyat Of Omar Khayyam** *by Edward Fitzgerald*	ISBN:*1-59462-332-5*	**$13.95**
	Edward Fitzgerald, whom the world has already learned, in spite of his own efforts to remain within the shadow of anonymity, to look upon as one of the rarest poets of the century, was born at Bredfield, in Suffolk, on the 31st of March, 1809. He was the third son of John Purcell...	Music Pages 172	
☐	**Ancient Law** *by Henry Maine*	ISBN: *1-59462-128-4*	**$29.95**
	The chief object of the following pages is to indicate some of the earliest ideas of mankind, as they are reflected in Ancient Law, and to point out the relation of those ideas to modern thought.	Religion/History Pages 452	
☐	**Far-Away Stories** *by William J. Locke*	ISBN: *1-59462-129-2*	**$19.45**
	"Good wine needs no bush, but a collection of mixed vintages does. And this book is just such a collection. Some of the stories I do not want to remain buried for ever in the museum files of dead magazine-numbers an author's not unpardonable vanity..."	Fiction Pages 272	
☐	**Life of David Crockett** *by David Crockett*	ISBN: *1-59462-250-7*	**$27.45**
	"Colonel David Crockett was one of the most remarkable men of the times in which he lived. Born in humble life, but gifted with a strong will, an indomitable courage, and unremitting perseverance...	Biographies/New Age Pages 424	
☐	**Lip-Reading** *by Edward Nitchie*	ISBN: *1-59462-206-X*	**$25.95**
	Edward B. Nitchie, founder of the New York School for the Hard of Hearing, now the Nitchie School of Lip-Reading, Inc, wrote "LIP-READING Principles and Practice". The development and perfecting of this meritorious work on lip-reading was an undertaking...	How-to Pages 400	
☐	**A Handbook of Suggestive Therapeutics, Applied Hypnotism, Psychic Science**	ISBN: *1-59462-214-0*	**$24.95**
	*by **Henry Munro***	Health/New Age/Health/Self-help Pages 376	
☐	**A Doll's House: and Two Other Plays** *by Henrik Ibsen*	ISBN: *1-59462-112-8*	**$19.95**
	Henrik Ibsen created this classic when in revolutionary 1848 Rome. Introducing some striking concepts in playwriting for the realist genre, this play has been studied the world over.	Fiction/Classics/Plays 308	
☐	**The Light of Asia** *by sir Edwin Arnold*	ISBN: *1-59462-204-3*	**$13.95**
	In this poetic masterpiece, Edwin Arnold describes the life and teachings of Buddha. The man who was to become known as Buddha to the world was born as Prince Gautama of India but he rejected the worldly riches and abandoned the reigns of power when...	Religion/History/Biographies Pages 170	
☐	**The Complete Works of Guy de Maupassant** *by Guy de Maupassant*	ISBN: *1-59462-157-8*	**$16.95**
	"For days and days, nights and nights, I had dreamed of that first kiss which was to consecrate our engagement, and I knew not on what spot I should put my lips..."	Fiction/Classics Pages 240	
☐	**The Art of Cross-Examination** *by Francis L. Wellman*	ISBN: *1-59462-309-0*	**$26.95**
	Written by a renowned trial lawyer, Wellman imparts his experience and uses case studies to explain how to use psychology to extract desired information through questioning.	How-to/Science/Reference Pages 408	
☐	**Answered or Unanswered?** *by Louisa Vaughan*	ISBN: *1-59462-248-5*	**$10.95**
	Miracles of Faith in China	Religion Pages 112	
☐	**The Edinburgh Lectures on Mental Science (1909)** *by Thomas*	ISBN: *1-59462-008-3*	**$11.95**
	This book contains the substance of a course of lectures recently given by the writer in the Queen Street Hail, Edinburgh. Its purpose is to indicate the Natural Principles governing the relation between Mental Action and Material Conditions...	New Age/Psychology Pages 148	
☐	**Ayesha** *by H. Rider Haggard*	ISBN: *1-59462-301-5*	**$24.95**
	Verily and indeed it is the unexpected that happens! Probably if there was one person upon the earth from whom the Editor of this, and of a certain previous history, did not expect to hear again...	Classics Pages 380	
☐	**Ayala's Angel** *by Anthony Trollope*	ISBN: *1-59462-352-X*	**$29.95**
	The two girls were both pretty, but Lucy who was twenty-one who supposed to be simple and comparatively unattractive, whereas Ayala was credited, as her Bombwhat romantic name might show, with poetic charm and a taste for romance. Ayala when her father died was nineteen...	Fiction Pages 484	
☐	**The American Commonwealth** *by James Bryce*	ISBN: *1-59462-286-8*	**$34.45**
	An interpretation of American democratic political theory. It examines political mechanics and society from the perspective of Scotsman James Bryce	Politics Pages 572	
☐	**Stories of the Pilgrims** *by Margaret P. Pumphrey*	ISBN: *1-59462-116-0*	**$17.95**
	This book explores pilgrims religious oppression in England as well as their escape to Holland and eventual crossing to America on the Mayflower, and their early days in New England...	History Pages 268	

QTY

The Fasting Cure *by Sinclair Upton*   ISBN: *1-59462-222-1*   **$13.95**

In the Cosmopolitan Magazine for May, 1910, and in the Contemporary Review (London) for April, 1910, I published an article dealing with my experiences in fasting. I have written a great many magazine articles, but never one which attracted so much attention...   *New Age/Self Help/Health Pages 164*

Hebrew Astrology *by Sepharial*   ISBN: *1-59462-308-2*   **$13.45**

In these days of advanced thinking it is a matter of common observation that we have left many of the old landmarks behind and that we are now pressing forward to greater heights and to a wider horizon than that which represented the mind-content of our progenitors...   *Astrology Pages 144*

Thought Vibration or The Law of Attraction in the Thought World   ISBN: *1-59462-127-6*   **$12.95**

by William Walker Atkinson   *Psychology/Religion Pages 144*

Optimism *by Helen Keller*   ISBN: *1-59462-108-X*   **$15.95**

Helen Keller was blind, deaf, and mute since 19 months old, yet famously learned how to overcome these handicaps, communicate with the world, and spread her lectures promoting optimism. An inspiring read for everyone...   *Biographies/Inspirational Pages 84*

Sara Crewe *by Frances Burnett*   ISBN: *1-59462-360-0*   **$9.45**

In the first place, Miss Minchin lived in London. Her home was a large, dull, tall one, in a large, dull square, where all the houses were alike, and all the sparrows were alike, and where all the door-knockers made the same heavy sound...   *Childrens/Classic Pages 88*

The Autobiography of Benjamin Franklin *by Benjamin Franklin*   ISBN: *1-59462-135-7*   **$24.95**

The Autobiography of Benjamin Franklin has probably been more extensively read than any other American historical work, and no other book of its kind has had such ups and downs of fortune. Franklin lived for many years in England, where he was agent...   *Biographies/History Pages 332*

Name	
Email	
Telephone	
Address	
City, State ZIP	

☐ **Credit Card**   ☐ **Check / Money Order**

Credit Card Number	
Expiration Date	
Signature	

Please Mail to: Book Jungle
PO Box 2226
Champaign, IL 61825
or Fax to: 630-214-0564

www.ingramcontent.com/pod-product-compliance
Lightning Source LLC
Chambersburg PA
CBHW080748250626

47162CB00010B/3057